He couldn't bear to think of harm coming to her.

She handed the gun back to him, almost reluctantly. "I could never be comfortable with it," she said. "When I'm afraid, I can't think. I can only feel, only be afraid." She glanced away. "But later, after the fear goes away, I start thinking. I think about having a gun like yours. I dream of having your courage, your confidence, your body."

McQuade swallowed hard and told himself that she hadn't really meant what she'd just said. After last night, he certainly wanted to have *her* body. But there was more to it than that. It was getting hard to handle the growing urge to shield her with his own body and protect her from the world.

He searched for a remark to cover himself, and he found a cocky grin to go with it. "That's why you hired me, honey. Don't go wishing for a man's body. Yours is great just the way it is."

Dear Reader,

Welcome to summer, and welcome to another fine month of reading from Silhouette Intimate Moments. We have some exciting books in store for you, not just this month, but all summer long. Let me start with our June titles, then give you a peek at what's coming up in the future.

First, there's *That McKenna Woman*, the first book in Parris Afton Bonds' Mescalero Trilogy. Parris used her home state of New Mexico as the location of the Mescalero Cattle Company, then peopled the ranch with some of the most charismatic characters you'll ever find. Tom Malcolm and Marianna McKenna couldn't be less alike, but that doesn't stop them from discovering a love as big as the West. And the family created by their marriage provides the basis for the other two books in the series, books we know you'll look forward to reading.

Another special book for June is Kathleen Eagle's *More Than a Miracle*, a follow-up to *Candles in the Night* (Silhouette Special Edition #437). This is the story of a woman who, forced to give up her child, now embarks on a desperate mission to find her son. Her only help comes from the man they call McQuade, and even then, it may take more than a miracle to make her dream come true.

During the rest of the summer, look for books by old favorites like Lucy Hamilton (whose Dodd Memorial Hospital Trilogy ends in July with *Heartbeats*), Heather Graham Pozzessere and Emilie Richards. They're just a few of the writers whose work will be waiting for you— only in the pages of Silhouette Intimate Moments.

Sincerely,

Leslie J. Wainger
Senior Editor, Silhouette Books

Kathleen Eagle

More Than a Miracle

Silhouette Intimate Moments

Published by Silhouette Books New York

America's Publisher of Contemporary Romance

SILHOUETTE BOOKS
300 East 42nd St., New York, N.Y. 10017

ISBN: 0-373-07242-2

First Silhouette Books printing June 1988

KATHLEEN EAGLE

is a transplant from Massachusetts to her favorite regional setting, the Dakota prairie. As educator, wife, mother and writer, she believes that a woman's place is wherever she's needed—and anywhere she needs to be.

For Christopher—
Thanks to my youngest,
I'm never at a loss
for hugs and kisses.

Chapter 1

McQuade stood on the landing and surveyed the crowd beneath the Purple Parrot's whirling ceiling fan. It was a mixed bag of locals and tourists, who were easily distinguished by their pink flamingo T-shirts with *Miami* splashed across the top. This wasn't a place he would have chosen for a meeting, but the woman involved had offered no choices.

He'd seen her only once before, and from that memory he was able to spot her immediately. She softened the space around her, creating her own niche of translucent blue-white in the middle of the smoky violet atmosphere. Her booth near the end of the bar was a little island, a haven at the edge of the din. McQuade wondered whether her isolation was self-imposed, or whether the boundaries were generally obvious and universally respected. It occurred to him that he might be the fool rushing in where wise men from near and far feared to tread.

The only reason he'd agreed to this meeting was that Mikal Romanov had called and asked him to. He would even give some consideration to taking whatever job the woman offered him, just because Mike had asked him to hear her out. Mike was the only true humanitarian McQuade had ever met, and the only man he ever did favors for. Otherwise his services were costly, and he wondered whether this woman could afford him.

McQuade drew a pack of cigarettes from the pocket of his denim jacket, shook one out and stuck it in his mouth. If he'd waited until he got to her table he would have had to ask. He was capable of being at least that civilized. Something told him she would have been gracious about it. She was the kind of woman who seemed to float several feet above everyone else, and what the teeming masses did would not affect her. He drew deeply on the cigarette and squinted through the smoke, thinking he would take his time and size her up from here.

She looked up, saw him and knew him instantly. She offered no cheery wave, no beckoning hand. Huge brown eyes dominated her face, and her gaze was riveting. For a moment he was back on the small, troubled island of De Colores, where he'd seen her in the cool of the Caribbean morning nearly a year ago. They hadn't spoken when he'd helped her with her bags as she and four other hostages of the island's new government were escorted to their plane.

The other hostages had been American, but she was a native of the island and had been headed for exile. The aloof dignity of her bearing had set her apart. It was common knowledge that her husband, a member of the new three-man junta, was sending her away, but beyond that information, no one had discussed her situation. Little was said to her, mostly because no one had the proper words to give her, but also because her proud bearing had invited no questions, no expressions of sympathy.

McQuade watched her and wondered when she would look away. He could almost always evoke a revealing reaction from a woman right from the start, simply by staring. Within fifteen seconds he could usually tell what she wanted from him. He watched her while he took another long, slow drag on his cigarette, but her expression remained unchanged. She, too, was watching.

He made his way to her table, pausing at the corner of the bar to crush his cigarette out in an ashtray. She kept track of him every step of the way, a tactic that made the skin on the back of his neck crawl, because it was one he normally used himself.

Taken off balance, he did something that was unusual for him; he offered what he thought would probably pass for a friendly smile as he extended his hand. "Mrs. Guerrero? I'm McQuade."

The smile she returned was tentative and didn't quite reach her wary eyes. She offered her hand. "Please sit

down, Mr. McQuade. I am Elizabeth Donnelly now.
I am divorced.''

"Donnelly?'' He knew of a Donnelly who'd had
some dealings in the islands, and as he extended a firm
handshake he promised himself that if she was related to *that* Donnelly, he would promptly tell her
goodbye, even though he found his fingers lingering
around hers. Her hand was slight and cold and seemed
to need his warmth. Before the moment became awk-
ward, he slid into the booth beside her.

"Yes,'' she said, confirming his suspicions with the
word. "My maiden name carries almost as many
thorns as my married name.''

"Why didn't you change it altogether, then?'' He
turned to find the bartender standing by his shoulder,
and he ordered bourbon and water. The man didn't
move until Elizabeth asked for a glass of white wine
and gave him a nod. "Your bodyguard?'' McQuade
asked after the bartender had moved on.

"My friend,'' she said. "And to answer your question, it wouldn't matter what my name was. My father was convicted of drug trafficking, and my ex-
husband is part of the new military government of De
Colores, so I'm well-known to any and all authori-
ties.''·She gave him a level stare. "And to answer the
question you haven't asked, I had nothing to do with
my father's business and very little to do with my father. Mikal Romanov was able to convince the U.S.
government of that fact. I've been granted political
asylum, and I've applied for citizenship. My mother
was, of course, De Coloran, my father American. The

island was apparently a convenient place from which to do business, and my mother and I were... conveniences, too."

"He got sent up about two years ago, didn't he?" She nodded. "Is your mother still on the island?"

"No. She's dead." The look she gave him constituted a dare. "Am I too hot to handle, Mr. McQuade?"

He laughed. It was such a funny phrase coming from her, especially when he thought of her cold hand. "You may well be, Miss Donnelly. You may very well be."

"I had hoped that Mikal Romanov and Freedom International would be able to take care of this for me. They freed us, you know, those of us who were detained after the coup. Mikal gave me your name the last time I called him. He said he'd done all he could."

McQuade remembered Mike's call the previous day. "She's got a plan that's right up your alley, McQuade. Real cloak-and-dagger stuff. Freedom International can't really touch the problem, because there are no prisoners involved anymore."

Because Mikal Romanov was the man he was, McQuade surmised that he himself was this woman's last resort. Mikal preferred to use diplomatic methods, while nobody had ever accused McQuade of being diplomatic. Freedom International worked for the discharge of political prisoners, and Mikal had done a beautiful job of negotiating the release of the hostages on De Colores after the sudden military coup that had taken place there a year before. McQuade figured he was about to hear of a problem that diplomatic methods had failed to solve.

"What do you want from me, Miss Donnelly?"

"I want a miracle, Mr. McQuade."

McQuade raised an eyebrow. He'd been called the miracle worker by some because his business was, among other things, finding missing people, and he'd been known to "raise the dead." If the lost were anywhere on God's green earth, chances were McQuade could find them, or, at the very least, find out what had become of them. He considered private detective agency to be too mundane a term to describe his business, so he was listed in the phone book simply as McQuade, Inc.—the Inc. for tax purposes. His clients were always referrals who came to him from any number of sources.

Lovely as this woman was, she was still a prospective client, and McQuade was a man who put first things first. "Miracles don't come cheap, Miss Donnelly."

"I can pay you," she told him.

"Pay me for what?"

"Guerrero has our son—*my* son. I want him back."

"Get in touch with General Castillo. Of the three honchos, he's got the final word there on De Colores, and he strikes me as a fairly sentimental old guy. Tell him—"

"You haven't heard, then. The general died of heart failure two days ago. It's just the two of them now. Miguel Hidalgo has taken charge of health, education, welfare of the people and internal matters, while—''

"There! That's even better. Hidalgo's a good man. He'll listen—''

"—while Guerrero commands all transportation, all military forces and all police.''

McQuade considered the information for a moment, remembering Guerrero, a man who wouldn't be satisfied until he'd armed every schoolboy on the island and taught them all to goose-step. "You're asking for more than a miracle, Miss Donnelly.''

"I've tried the Red Cross, the State Department, even the Church. They tell me that this is a family matter, that Guerrero is a father with legal custody. Custody! Who determined that?'' Her soft brown eyes suddenly hardened. "We will have to kidnap my son.''

McQuade gave a short bark of laughter. Not that the request was funny, nor was it the first time he'd heard it. He'd run into a hundred kinds of desperation in his line of work. He'd run into a hundred kinds of madmen, too, and he'd judged Colonel Rodolfo Guerrero to be one of the worst he'd seen. This woman had to be Mrs. Madman, divorced or not. With Guerrero in charge, the presidential palace at La Primavera, the island's capital, would undoubtedly be a well-armed military compound by now.

His laugh drew an icy stare from the lady. "Mikal Romanov recommended you highly, Mr. McQuade. I'm surprised you lack the courtesy to even take my predicament seriously.''

He moved his arm aside as his drink was delivered to the table, and he waved her complaint away after he'd paid the bartender, whose stare was as cold as Elizabeth's. The whole situation was thin-ice territory, McQuade decided. "Look, I wasn't laughing at your predicament, but you'll have to admit that the idea of kidnapping Guerrero's son is a little—"

"_My_ son," Elizabeth repeated.

"Guerrero's his father, right? You just admitted that." The woman nodded solemnly. "And since he's half the government down there, he decides who's got custody. I guess I assumed you had a deal when you left—you got your freedom, he got the kid."

"When it was decided to release the other hostages, Guerrero ordered me to leave. I was not allowed to take my son."

Once again he saw the tragic dignity he'd noticed in her face the day she'd left the island. Her dark eyes were clouded with pain, but she held her pointed little patrician chin high. He couldn't imagine why any man would mind having her satin slippers stashed under his bed.

"Why'd he kick you out?"

It was Elizabeth's turn to laugh, but her amusement was brief. She took a sip of her wine and shook her head as she swallowed it. "It's a very long story, Mr. McQuade, one that would bore you, I'm sure. I was more than pleased to terminate my relationship with Guerrero, but I had hoped to be allowed to live quietly with my son near La Primavera, in the house

where I was born. Guerrero decided to take my home
and my son from me because I am not . . ."

He waited for her to finish, interested in knowing
just what she was not. When it finally appeared that
she'd decided against telling him, he prodded. "You're
not what?"

There was a hint of defiance in her eyes as she
straightened her shoulders. "According to Guerrero,
I'm not one of the people his so-called government
represents. My mother was, in his words, an aristo-
crat, and my father is an American criminal." She
gave another mirthless little laugh. "All Americans
have become criminals in Guerrero's eyes, but in my
father's case—" she shrugged "—it's actually true."

"So why did he marry you?"

"Times and Guerrero's fortunes were quite different five years ago."

His real question was why had *she* married *him*, but
he would let that one go. He found himself feeling a
greater measure of sympathy for her than he'd
planned to allow himself. Get the facts, weigh the
odds, and take the job or leave it, he told himself.

McQuade leaned back and rolled his half-empty
glass between his palms. "I guess you know how particular they've gotten about who gets on and off that
island," he said.

"I wouldn't be able to enter the country by ordi-
nary means anyway. We would have to—"

He glanced up quickly. "Lady, if I took this job,
you wouldn't be able to go, period."

"If you took this job," she said quietly, "I would accompany you. That would be a requirement."

"When I take a job, I determine the requirements."

They stared at each other with firm conviction. "We are talking of my son, Mr. McQuade. He is only two years old. I will not have him taken from his home and smuggled to this country by a stranger."

"Then you probably won't have him at all, Miss Donnelly. It won't be a piece of cake, getting him out of that compound, and you won't find—"

"I have a plan."

"You look like you have a plan. And I look like a Boy Scout whose motto is Be Prepared for Ladies Who Have Plans." Wit like that called for another drink, and McQuade signaled the bartender.

Elizabeth frowned as she bit back words. She needed this man's help, and she wouldn't get it by telling him what she thought of his smug attitude. The words would keep until she had her son back. Mikal Romanov had assured her that she could trust McQuade, and Elizabeth held Mikal's recommendation in high regard, despite the chauvinistic smirk on the face she was carefully surveying. It was chiseled, with an angular jaw, a slightly irregular nose that might once have been broken, and gray eyes. There was no mistaking his masculinity, and Elizabeth didn't doubt that he had a typically masculine ego to match. She decided she could work that ego to her advantage for a change.

"I don't think you look like a Boy Scout, Mr. McQuade." She turned toward him, bracing her elbow near the edge of the table, and touched two fingers to her chin as she appraised him. "You look like a risk-taker. A man like you makes his own plans when a lucrative opportunity presents itself. You strike me as a man who's prepared to challenge the odds if the rewards promise to be worthwhile."

She was a classic. McQuade took a quick mental review of the women he'd known in the past, but he couldn't recall feminine poise that could rival hers. Worse, he couldn't call up the features of any other face as he looked at hers. She was a classic, all right. He summoned every ounce of cockiness he could muster.

"What's your offer, Miss Donnelly?"

"Ten thousand in advance. Forty when my son and I are safely back in the United States."

"That's only money." The look he gave her was loaded with other suggestions.

"Yes, it is," she said calmly. "If you thrive on adventure, I'm sure this job will provide you with that, also."

McQuade chuckled as he plucked a purple book of matches from the ashtray on the table. "Money and adventure, huh? You add bourbon, broads, cigarettes and rare steak to the list, and I start thriving pretty well."

"I'm sure fifty thousand dollars will go a long way, Mr. McQuade. Those things are all for sale." She gave him a pointed stare. "Are you?"

"I'm for hire, Miss Donnelly, when a job feels right to me. So far, this one doesn't fit. It feels tight." He bunched his shoulders in a gesture that suggested he felt constrained by his jacket, which was actually neatly tailored for his broad build. "Will we have to stop at the bank in La Primavera to make a withdrawal before we make our getaway?"

"I have the money, Mr. McQuade. And I bank in Switzerland."

"Don't we all? How'd you manage to keep Guerrero's hands off your money?"

"My mother did, actually, though her concern when she set up the trust fund for me was to keep my father's hands off the money—*her* family's money. When I reached the age of twenty-one, I allowed Guerrero to use some of my inheritance, but I had the sense to shelter the rest of it. He didn't realize that." She smiled, taking satisfaction in her small victory, but McQuade seemed unimpressed with her foresight. He must have enjoyed so many small victories that he couldn't appreciate this one, she thought. But she knew what he would appreciate. "I do have the money."

The arrival of another drink for McQuade and a second glass of wine for Elizabeth eased the moment. After a couple of quiet sips she asked, "Don't you want to hear my plan?"

McQuade settled back. Elizabeth Donnelly was easy to look at, and his second drink was sliding down even slicker than the first. "Why the hell not? Let's have it."

"I've arranged for a private plane."

McQuade acknowledged this by raising his eyebrows. "Nice. Where do we land this plane?"

"I'm not sure. I thought you'd probably have some ideas on that."

"Mmm. I even get to have ideas. Okay, so we land this plane somewhere. Then what?"

Elizabeth lifted a slender hand. "Then I have relatives, friends who will give us refuge. We'll make our way toward the palace."

"Umm-hmm."

"And you'll slip in . . . under cover of darkness."

"Oh, yeah, I've seen that done."

"If Tomás has the same nurse . . ."

"Tomás. That's the kid."

"Yes. If he still has the same nurse, she'll help us. I'm sure she'll still be there. Guerrero doesn't realize that she's my great-aunt."

"That's a plus."

"You'll bring him out, and we'll make our way back to the plane, or possibly to a boat, and we'll . . ."

McQuade's brow was furrowed, but amusement made his mouth twitch. "I think there are some holes in this plan, Miss Donnelly."

"And I think fifty thousand dollars should plug them up." Her smile was a mere wisp. McQuade wasn't quite sure he could even call it a smile, except that there was a sudden hopeful sheen in her eyes. He wondered whether she really believed money had that much power. "I can understand why your services come dear," Elizabeth added smoothly. "Mikal Romanov said he knew of no one else who knows the island, is familiar with the palace and has the expertise that you have.''

She was making him sound as good as he was beginning to feel. He wondered how much of that had to do with her and how much had to do with his second drink, which was turning out to be a real kicker. "What kind of expertise did Mike credit me with?"

She lifted one shoulder and waved a hand to indicate that he surely must have been aware of his reputation. "A lot of local connections, a bloodhound's nose, an ability to defend yourself and others, the kind of cunning that—"

McQuade laughed. "Good God, why don't they make a movie about me! I sound terrific.''

"He said you're the best there is, and that's what I need. You helped Mrs. Romanov.''

He remembered how Mike's new wife had looked when she'd come to McQuade's cubbyhole of an office on the island, trying to find someone to get her into the palace to see Mike. Morgan Kramer had had *teacher* written all over her face and *woman beside herself with worry over her man* etched in her eyes. McQuade had been working with the Red Cross and Freedom International at the time, locating people who'd gotten lost in the shuffle of the coup, but he'd been able to dig up some information for several clients of his own in the process. With the Red Cross it was charity, and with Mike it was friendship, but he was also in this business for profit. And this woman was offering . . .

"Fifty thousand, huh?" He raised his glass, eyeing her over the rim as he took another drink. Best damned bourbon he'd ever tasted, and, if anything, the lady's bartender friend had skimped on the water.

"It's *respectable* money, Mr. McQuade. As I've explained, I inherited it from my mother."

"I'm not real fussy about where you got your money, lady, as long as it was printed by the U.S. Treasury Department." The bartender replaced McQuade's empty glass with a full one. McQuade flashed a questioning glance at Elizabeth. "Did you order this?"

"On the house, sir." The burly man took the white dish towel off his shoulder and took a swipe at the ring of water on the table. "The lady's a good customer."

McQuade made a point of surveying the Purple Parrot, from the gaudy papier-mâché bird that hung over the bar to the cashier, whose black-and-orange jungle-print sheath was backless to the waist. He raised an eyebrow at Elizabeth as he slid his complimentary drink back and forth over the pockmarked wooden table. "Strange hangout for a lady."

Elizabeth's survey took the same path as Mc-Quade's. The place offered her the kind of distraction she needed. There were people everywhere. She didn't know them, but they were there, and that was something. She looked back to find McQuade staring at her oddly. "I don't know anyone in Miami," she explained. "As soon as I have my son, I'll probably move to New England. I went to school there, and it's the only part of the country I know. But for now..."

Her thoughts drifted away, and McQuade felt strangely bereft. He wanted her to talk to him. "Where are you staying?" he asked.

She smiled. Perhaps the question indicated a spark of interest in her situation. She sensed that so far he'd been put off by the mere fact that she was who she was. "I've taken an apartment and part-time job tutoring immigrants in English. Matt, the bartender, lives in my building."

McQuade glanced back over his shoulder and caught one of the many stares he knew had been trained on him since he'd sat down. He waved a single finger at the dusky-eyed man, who turned away without responding.

"I think he'd sooner break both my legs than serve me free drinks," McQuade decided.

"He's been a good friend to me," Elizabeth said quietly. "He wouldn't harm a fly."

McQuade nodded, smiling as he pictured the big bartender armed with a flyswatter. "Sure. Unless that fly came buzzing around you. Why don't you take Matt to De Colores and send him into Guerrero's little fortress?"

"He's offered to do that. If you think you need another man, I could ask him to come along."

"Instead of you?"

"No. I intend to go with you, regardless."

"I wouldn't need another man, and I certainly wouldn't need to drag you along, either. A job like this is best done quickly and quietly by a single person who knows how to handle himself.'' His hard look challenged her to argue with the sense of that.

"I would follow your directions, Mr. McQuade. I'd help, I'd stay out of your way—whatever you said. But no power on earth could keep me from going with you."

He saw her resolve in the way she clasped her hands in her lap and squared her shoulders. She had a slight build, somewhat tall—willowy, he decided. She had a strong will going for her, and she was determined to find her son. Hiring some muscle seemed to be important to her. She'd need some firepower, too, considering who she was up against. McQuade figured a flyswatter would be about all the firepower Matt, the bartender, could handle. He tossed back the rest of his drink and decided that Matt did, however, have a way with bourbon.

McQuade set his glass down and leaned forward. "Look, I'll give this some thought, Miss Donnelly. I want to talk to some people, find out what really happened to Castillo and what's going on down there now that he's out of the picture, see what my chances are of getting on that island without being noticed—details like that. I'll give you my answer in a couple of days."

"I'd like to leave tomorrow."

She had a delicate way of being demanding. McQuade saw the hunger in her eyes and knew that she was fighting to cover it up. She was striving for a look of serene dignity, one that said nothing could touch her. It wasn't working, but McQuade couldn't take much pleasure in that fact. The look in her eyes was having too strong an effect on him. He glanced away and noticed that another drink had appeared at his elbow.

"I can't believe the service around here," McQuade mumbled, tasting it. "Again the good stuff."

"Matt knows I need your help," Elizabeth explained. "It must be his way of saying— What's wrong, Mr. McQuade?"

He scowled at the drink in his hand for a moment, then carefully placed it on the table as though it might have a life of its own. Then he turned hooded gray eyes on Elizabeth. "Tomorrow's too soon. Listen, company's been great, proposal's interesting, can't ask for more than drinks on the house, but I have to think it over." He slid out of the booth abruptly and offered his hand. "I've got your number. I'll give you a call."

Stunned, Elizabeth watched McQuade thread his way among tables and people as he headed for the door, walking a little less fluidly than he had when he'd come in. He tipped over one empty chair, caught it and set it back, then moved on.

"Where's he headed?"

Elizabeth looked up to find Matt, his arms folded around his barrel chest, glowering after the retreating McQuade.

"I don't know. All of a sudden he'd heard enough."

Matt shifted a toothpick from one side of his mouth to the other and made a clucking sound as he watched the door close behind the man Miss Donnelly wanted to hire. "If you'd 'a kept him here a little longer, I'd 'a had him passed out cold, and you could 'a dumped him in the plane and taken him where you wanted him.''

"What?"

Matt grinned at the lady's wide-eyed shock. "He won't get far as it is. Surprises me he could walk out like that. Hope he's not driving."

"Matt!" Elizabeth shot out of the booth and grabbed her purse. "Did you put something in his drinks?"

"It's an old recipe, Miss Donnelly, nothing—"

"Not drugs," she hissed. "You didn't—"

"It's just booze," Matt said with a shrug. "Goes down easy, but . . ."

Matt grinned as he watched Elizabeth shoulder her way through the crowd. If Mr. McQuade was still on his feet, he was about to have himself an embarrassing moment in front of Miss Donnelly.

Out on the sidewalk, Elizabeth frantically scanned the street for McQuade. Oh, God, she thought, he's gotten behind the wheel. Then she spotted him across the street. On slightly unsteady legs, he was headed for the wharf. She gave the traffic only a cursory glance before she hiked her straight skirt above her knees and made a headlong dash across the road.

Squealing brakes and the scream of a horn pulled McQuade's head around. Whatever he'd been drinking sure played hell with the mind, he told himself. Through the headlights he thought he saw a gorgeous pair of legs and Elizabeth Donnelly's face. What was in between was blotted out by glare until another car skidded to a stop and she sprinted past it. God, yes, Elizabeth Donnelly, skirt up around her thighs and running across the street, looking incredibly graceful and long legged.

"You're gonna get killed!" he shouted, and a man in a cab yelled something about where he was going to leave his tire marks. McQuade responded in kind, feeling in the right mood to shout down even a cab-driver. He reached for Elizabeth and hauled her over the curb as the cab whizzed by. "What the hell are you—"

"You mustn't drive, Mr. McQuade," she gasped, grabbing the front of his denim jacket for support.

"You think I don't know that? I need some air first. That's some drink your buddy, Matt..." Gripping her arms, he pulled her face closer to his. "What the hell— I can't believe I let you slip me something, lady."

"I didn't. I swear it. Please, let's walk, Mr. Mc-Quade. Unless you feel—"

"What was I drinking?" He tightened his grip and the terror that flashed in her eyes surprised him. "Just tell me," he said evenly.

"Matt said it was just liquor, some kind of recipe. He wouldn't hurt you, I'm sure of it. He was trying to help me."

"By getting me drunk? What for?"

She shook her head, and her long dark hair swished about her shoulders. "I guess he thought it would be easier to get you on the plane that way. I'm sorry, Mr. McQuade. Matt didn't mean any harm.''

He released her slowly, but she continued to stare at him, wide-eyed, like a night creature mesmerized by headlights. "I think I just need some air," he told her. "I'm gonna walk out on the pier for a minute.''

She watched him stumble twice on the steps that would take him from street level to the wharf. He'd fall in the water, she told herself, and she hurried after him. "Let me go with you, Mr. McQuade," she called.

He turned and waited while he put a cigarette in his mouth and struck a match.

"Did you come in your own car?'' she asked, approaching him cautiously. He had a right to be angry, she realized, and anyway, anger was what she had learned to expect from men.

"Yeah. Parked it in a lot. Hate to leave it in a lot down here overnight, but since I don't know what in hell it was I drank..." He blew a steam of gray smoke and started toward the pier. It was quiet down there. Maybe his head would clear.

"I'll drive you home, Mr. McQuade.''

He turned to her, and she stopped in her tracks. She stood there, looking up at him in the lamplight, her chest fluttering with the unsteadiness of her breathing. She was scared, and McQuade wasn't sure whether the dash across the street was the cause or whether he was. Yet she had offered to drive him home. "Then how would you get where you're going?'' he asked.

"I'd take a taxi."

"You've got a driver's license?"

"Of course."

He smiled at her bravado. "I don't want to be inside anything right now," he told her honestly. "Especially not something that moves. How about sitting out on the pier with me for a little while? Looking at the lights?"

She brushed at her skirt and then squared her shoulders, once again the lady with poise. "That would be very nice."

They found a spot where they could sit in near darkness and listen to the water lap at the sides of the boats moored nearby. A bridge stretched over the bay, and its lights were draped in scallop formation across the sky. McQuade finished his cigarette in silence, then flicked it into the water.

"I think I could get to the island myself," Elizabeth mused aloud. "They got Mrs. Romanov out of the palace by disguising her. Maybe I could get in the same way."

McQuade swung his head around and looked at her. She was staring off across the water, and he knew her brain was ticking in high gear. "You'd try it, wouldn't you? You'd give it a shot on your own."

She turned to him. "My son was just toddling when I saw him last. He only knew a few words. He might not even . . . know me right away."

"Is Matt's recipe for sale?" he wondered. "I've got some friends I'd like to try it on." His smile came slowly. "Your ex-husband, for one."

"You'll help me, then?"

McQuade sighed. This was another look he couldn't resist. Woman beside herself with worry over her kid. "A boy oughta be with his mother," he said quietly.

"Tomorrow?" she asked, brightening there in the dark.

"Not tomorrow, honey." He chuckled. "I'm going to have a record-breaking headache, so I'm gonna have to turn you down for tomorrow."

"I could drive you to the airport, Mr. McQuade, and you could sleep all the way to—"

"I can't be ready by morning, Elizabeth. I really have to check some things out before I jump into this."

"But the plane—"

"You let me talk to your pilot. I don't think I want to fly directly to De Colores, anyway. I'm gonna let you drive me home and pick me up in my car tomorrow. Then I'll meet this pilot of yours." He rolled his eyes toward the stars. "I hope he isn't related to your bartender."

Elizabeth smiled to herself, reserving her comments. "I'll have your advance ready tomorrow, Mr. McQuade."

He said nothing. He didn't want to discuss money with her now. He only hoped he could get off the pier without falling into the water. One more cigarette, he decided.

"Do you have a first name, Mr. McQuade?"

He drew deeply on the smoke and held it, then expelled it, remembering. "Yeah, but I never use it."

"May I?"

He shrugged. "Sure. It's Sloan."

She turned her face up to him, and in the dim light he saw that look again. She spoke in a pleading tone. "Help me get my son back, Sloan."

Chapter 2

Whoever the hell you are, you press that thing one more time and I'm coming down to break your finger."

Elizabeth drew her hand back from the buzzer as though she'd been burned, and then she checked her watch again. Hadn't he told her to pick him up in the morning? Eight o'clock was surely reasonable if he intended to get anything done today.

She stepped closer to the intercom and spoke quietly. "It's Elizabeth Donnelly, Mr. McQuade." Elizabeth tried to match her memory of McQuade's stony face to the agonized groan she was hearing over the intercom, but she couldn't get them to fit together. "I'm not too early, am I?"

"I take it you know what time it is."

"Yes, of course. I thought we should get started now."

"Oh, yeah?" The mirthless chuckle fit her picture of him well. "Come on up, then."

He was just another man, Elizabeth told herself as she stepped into the elevator. He couldn't help being so obnoxious, and she was prepared to be tolerant of simple obnoxiousness for Tomás's sake. Given the previous night's circumstances, he was probably even entitled to a few hours' foul mood. She would make it a point to be pleasant as long as he wasn't abusive. But the face that appeared at the apartment door after she knocked could have wilted a cactus. Elizabeth took a deep breath.

"I brought your car, Mr. McQuade. I wasn't sure how early you'd need it."

He gave her a cold, low-lidded stare. "Why the hell would I need a car? I've got my own freight train running through my head, thanks to Matt, the harmless bartender."

"I'll just leave these with you." She extended long fingers and a palm full of keys. The door swung open.

"Bring them in here so we can get on with whatever we're supposed to start in the middle of the night."

He stepped around the door, and she saw his white terry cloth bathrobe first, and then his bare feet. She wasn't sure why she wanted to giggle. "It's eight o'clock in the morning, Mr. McQuade."

"I resisted the urge to report that to you, Miss Donnelly. Do me the same favor."

"Perhaps if you had some coffee," she suggested as she stepped into the darkened room. The jacket he'd worn the previous night was lying on the carpet beside a leather chair.

"Perhaps if I went back to bed." He turned to raise one eyebrow at her, which took some effort. The skin grated over his skull. "Care to join me? I think I need to start this day all over again, with something more soothing than the sound of a doorbell buzzing." He managed part of a smile. "Can you think of anything?"

"Coddled eggs?"

His mouth turned down as he turned his back, grumbling, "Sounds slimy. You want coffee, you can make it. I'll be in the shower."

Elizabeth hoped he'd find that soothing. She opened the drapes and saw that the living room was in good order except for the clothes he'd shed the night before. She found the kitchen in good condition, too, with the makings for coffee stored in logical places. She didn't come across an abundance of groceries, but there was enough for a bacon-and-egg breakfast, and she proceeded to go to work. Sloan McQuade would be no good to her until his health was restored.

McQuade knew what the lady had cooking the minute he stepped out of the bathroom. It never bothered him when a woman got that domestic urge the morning after, but this wasn't a morning after. There was no feeling of exhilaration and no reason to believe he'd be welcome to walk up behind her and pat her bottom while she flipped his eggs. Worse yet, there was no reason to think his stomach wouldn't reject the eggs outright. He remembered what he'd gotten himself into the night before, but as he slipped into a pair of jeans, he couldn't remember why.

When he saw her standing in his kitchen with a plate of toast in one hand and a jar of jelly in the other, his memory came up with a flash of glaring headlights and beautiful legs. He watched as she gave the refrigerator door a nudge with her backside, and he knew this was the morning after a significant something had occurred. But he had the sinking feeling it was the beginning of something other than his customary after-breakfast farewells. With her long black hair, sleek as a seal's, setting off her soft white slacks and top, she seemed an unlikely domestic. More like an angel, he thought, then told himself to squelch such dangerous comparisons.

"So, Miss Donnelly, if you haven't made plans for breakfast, how about my place?"

Elizabeth turned, expecting to see him restored to the man she'd met the previous night, but his bare chest and faded jeans shocked away the pleasant answer she'd had ready for him. She stood in the middle of his apartment with his breakfast in her hands, and his smile said that he'd dressed with her in mind. His long, wiry torso looked hard and spare, which surprised her, because the simple lines of a shirt and jacket had softened him somewhat. She'd wanted him to be hard, of course, harder than Guerrero. She'd gone shopping for just such a man, and she hoped she'd found him, but that hardness—the stony face and those eyes and that chest—that hardness was as frightening to her as it was essential to him and his ability to do his job. Necessary for her, too, she reminded herself. She was going with him, and she, too, would have to be hard.

"Satisfied?"

Elizabeth raised her eyes to his, then looked away. He had an American smile; there was a playful hint of boy within the man. "I didn't mean to stare, Mr. McQuade, but that's an unsettling way to come to the table."

"I'm not unsettled. Are you?" He laughed, looking up at her with a mischievous twinkle in his eyes. "And I wasn't planning to come to the table, but make yourself at home. *Mi casa es su casa.*"

Elizabeth carried the toast and jelly to the table she'd already set, while three steps below her in the living room McQuade tossed his jacket on the sofa and plopped himself into the chair. "You speak Spanish, then," she said. She poured a cup of coffee and took it down to him.

"Not half as well as you speak English." He eyed the cup. "One sugar, no cream."

She took the coffee back up to the table, added his sugar, and put one piece of toast on a plate. Perhaps he'd start with that. "Do you take jelly on your toast?"

"Peanut butter, usually," he told her. It made him uneasy when she started for the kitchen. "But not today. Just that, that's fine. Really, that's all I can—" He accepted the coffee this time and set the plate of toast on a table beside him. "Look, I told you I'll take the job if I still think I can pull it off after I do a little checking. None of this is necessary. I'll make some calls, and I'll meet your pilot this afternoon. I promise."

"I asked Ronnie to meet us at the airport at nine-thirty. I thought you'd want to see the plane." She sat on the edge of the chair across from him and watched him sip his coffee. His wet hair was plastered against his head in tousled coils. "I thought you'd feel better if you ate something. I'm sorry about those drinks."

Her eyes were so wide with contrition, her face so pretty, that he was persuaded to reach for half a piece of toast just because she'd made it. "Guess I met my match. That stuff had one hell of a kick to it."

"I wouldn't have taken advantage of you, Mr. McQuade."

The idea made him laugh. He hoped she didn't expect the same nobility on his part, since they were about to spend a lot of time together, and that fresh flower scent she wore was making him want to follow his nose to whatever she'd dabbed it on.

"It's important to me that you believe that. I know I'm asking you to risk your life."

He saw how serious she was, and he decided to make it easier for her—and for himself, as well. "You're paying pretty well for it."

She nodded. "Would you like more coffee?"

"I think I'd like to watch you eat, too. What's on the menu besides coddled eggs?"

She smiled as she rose to her feet, and he knew he'd have to follow her to find out.

Ronnie Harper was not the man McQuade had expected. He wondered if she thought she was fooling anybody by shoving her pale red hair under a baseball cap. She wasn't going to make it as a man, and if she didn't get rid of those shapeless khaki shorts and high-top gym shoes she was liable to miss the mark as a woman. As it was, she could have passed for a Little Leaguer. McQuade offered her a nod and a handshake, but when Ronnie headed for her twin-engine Cessna, beckoning her prospective passengers to come aboard for a tour, McQuade grabbed Elizabeth by the elbow and grounded her where she stood.

"This *kid* is supposed to fly us to the island?" Elizabeth pulled her arm from his grasp, and he scowled as he leaned in closer. "It's bad enough that I have to take you along, but I'm not getting into this with some kid. We're not flying into a friendly situation, if you'll remember."

"I remember."

He closed his eyes and huffed. This woman had a way of looking at him that forced him to modify his worst retorts. "Okay, look." He laid a hand on her shoulder, but she chafed under that, too, so he shoved it into his pocket. "I'll look around for a plane, and I'll split the difference with you if I can't find as good a deal as you must have gotten on—"

"I've already hired her, Mr. McQuade, and I've paid her half in advance." She gave him a moment to

roll his eyes and make a gesture of frustration. "I've
spent months looking for a pilot. Most of them refuse to go near the island. Those who *are* willing want
to be paid a king's ransom in advance, and they remind me of people who worked for my father. I believe we can trust this woman."

They turned their heads toward the airplane. Ronnie Harper was sitting, chin in hand, in the open
doorway, watching.

"She doesn't look like the type to be running drugs
or illegal aliens," McQuade admitted, "but you can't
go by looks."

"She's flown Red Cross supplies into De Colores
with Miguel Hidalgo's blessing."

"What about Guerrero?"

Elizabeth laughed. "Blessings from Guerrero? Not
for St. Francis himself, Mr. McQuade."

The flash of mirth in her eyes was a nice change.
McQuade knew his resolve was softening. "She looks
like a kid," he repeated stubbornly.

"As you just said, you can't go by looks. She's
twenty-seven, she's been flying for eight years, and
she's logged hundreds of hours in the Caribbean. I've
investigated her thoroughly."

McQuade raised one eyebrow as he glanced at Elizabeth. He considered the plane again. "Thoroughly,
huh? We'll see." With a shrug, he started toward the
plane. "Let's get on with the interview."

McQuade's first meeting with Ronnie Harper convinced him that it was worth his while to consider her,
but an interview with her was only the beginning. As

always, he had some calls to make. After he dropped Elizabeth off at her apartment, he went about the business for which he was handsomely paid, though few clients knew the degree of care he took in checking all the angles. They paid him for results. This was how he got them and lived to tell about it.

Elizabeth Donnelly's apartment building didn't fit McQuade's image of her. He took the first three flights two steps at a time, but the last two flights slowed him down. On the way up he heard one squabble in English, two in Spanish and a chorus of crying babies. The island princess should have been spending her exile in a penthouse, preferably one with a limited-access elevator. She opened the door before he could knock twice.

"I was beginning to worry. I was afraid you'd changed your mind."

She had that fear in her eyes again, and McQuade stepped past her, resisting the niggling urge to reassure her with promises and other comforts. "The pilot's okay. I checked her out. I called a few people I thought might know something about Castillo's death, but it's all pretty vague. He did have a bad heart, and they're saying natural causes. Sounds like an uneasy partnership between Hidalgo and Guerrero."

"They are very different men."

Having moved inside, he turned to look at her in this unlikely setting. This was where she lived, in this sparsely furnished walk-up, but nothing of her was here. The white paint, brown carpet and red vinyl were not part of her; she could have been standing in some department store kitchen. She wore the soft white she seemed to favor, and her dark hair was caught up off her slender neck. She was white gardenias touched by an evening breeze. He suddenly realized he'd lost track of her last comment.

"Did you check me out, too?" she asked.

"Yeah. Yeah, I did." He glanced out the window, not bothered by the fact that he'd done his job, but embarrassed by what he'd been thinking and feeling a moment ago.

"Because of my father or my ex-husband?"

"Both."

"And are *you* satisfied?"

He turned to her and smiled. "You look okay to me. I went back and had a talk with Ronnie. We leave early in the morning."

"Before eight o'clock?"

"I'll pick you up at five. I've taken care of everything we need except your personal gear—whatever you can fit into a duffel bag." She nodded, and he felt good about the new expression in her eyes. He'd given her hope. "I'm changing the itinerary. We're flying into Arco Iris, and then we're taking a fishing boat from there."

"Why?" She'd sailed to the little island of Arco Iris many times. It was Mexican territory, but the two islands, De Colores to the west of Cuba and Arco Iris still farther west, shared the fishing waters between them.

"I don't want Ronnie to risk anything going in. A plane is more suspect than a fishing boat. She'll fly on to De Colores with her usual load of supplies for the Red Cross. We'll connect with her there, and she'll fly us out."

"How will we find a fisherman who's willing to take us?" She thought for a moment, then shook her head. "I might know someone in De Colores, but Arco Iris..."

"You leave that to me. I know people, too. That's why you hired me."

"It will take longer this way." She moved to the open window and looked down at the street. A group of small children were playing with a ball in the alley across the way. "I'd hoped we could be there tomorrow."

"The trick is to get there and back." He followed the direction of her gaze and watched, chuckling when one child bounced the ball off the back of another's head. "Looks like incubator alley down there. They sure have a lot of kids in this part of town."

"Don't you like children, Mr. McQuade?"

He shrugged. "Sure, I like kids. Who doesn't?"

"It's important to me that *you* do. I don't want my son left on that island under any circumstances." He turned to her and saw nothing of the fear he'd seen moments ago. Now her dark eyes burned with determination. "I'm paying you to see him safely away from De Colores and out of Guerrero's reach. I want to be sure you understand that."

Frowning in response to what appeared to be instructions for the feebleminded, he leaned one shoulder against the windowsill and folded his arms across his chest. "I understand what you've hired me to do, but I want you to understand something. You've complicated the job by insisting on coming along."

"I can't stay behind."

"You should also know that snatching a kid from his father can be sticky, and I've never tried it with a kid whose father is a head of state."

"But you have done this sort of thing before?"

He nodded. "For a woman who had custody, but the ex-husband skipped the country with the kid. You've got no custody, no laws on your side."

She turned away from him and watched the children again. She knew how bad the odds were; she didn't need to be reminded that she had no legal rights. In a way it bothered her that he was willing to help her. A man who could be bought, even at such a high price, could not be trusted. Yet if anything happened to her, she had to trust him with her son.

"Why didn't you move into a better neighborhood?" he asked. "This place isn't safe for a woman alone."

"My tutoring job pays the rent here," she told him. "I knew it might take everything I had to get my son back." Sparing him a sidelong glance, she added, "Especially since I have no laws on my side."

McQuade sighed as he straightened and stepped back from the window. Those eyes would be the death of him. "You've got me. What more can you ask?"

She smiled. "I'll be waiting at five."

McQuade arrived the next morning at the appointed time. He could tell she'd been up long before five. She was wide-eyed with anticipation, but she said little as they drove to the airport. McQuade felt as though he were accompanying a pilgrim on some holy journey, and he wished there was some way to protect her from her own high hopes. She'd followed his instructions by packing her personal items in a waterproof duffel bag, and she'd dressed in jeans and running shoes. She was ready to do the impossible, and determined that it would be done.

McQuade assigned Elizabeth to sit up front with Ronnie while he slept. He made a habit of sleeping when there was nothing better to do, and he judged that Elizabeth's adrenaline would keep her going for another twenty-four hours. When he woke, the women were chatting like old friends. He was glad Ronnie had gotten Elizabeth to relax.

"Arco Iris," Ronnie announced. Elizabeth leaned forward in her seat. They were making their descent, and the island had become a discernible dark spot in the blue sea.

"Look, Sloan! We're halfway there."

He'd begun to wonder whether she'd forgotten his name. Not that it mattered. McQuade was all anyone ever called him, even if that someone was whispering in his ear. But the sound of his given name made him sit up with a smile on his face.

"No kidding? This is a great little place," he said, searching out the spot for himself. "Nice beach, nice take-it-easy people."

"And at least one nice fisherman, I hope," Elizabeth wished aloud as she watched the island draw closer. "With a nice, fast boat."

The fisherman with the fast boat was not at the top of McQuade's priority list when he stepped off Ronnie's plane. He wanted a room, a shower and a stiff drink, which meant the first thing to do was look up Felix Santiago. Felix would grant those first three wishes instantly and immediately start locating the fisherman. All McQuade had to do was head for the Oyster Shell.

It was one of Arco Iris's three guest houses, and the sign above the front door proclaimed it a favorite haunt of Ernest Hemingway. The tiny lobby sported the obligatory ceiling fan, rattan furniture and mahogany reception desk, as well as a little old man whose black hair, slicked straight back from his face, gleamed with telltale hints of green. Felix Santiago did not plan to let his age show.

"I wasn't expecting you, McQuade. You don't tell me you're coming, I don't save your room." Felix shook a finger, but his eyes teased. "You should have let me know."

"This is just a quick trip, Felix. Anything you've got is okay." He dropped his big, green army duffel bag at the base of the desk.

Felix glanced at the two women standing behind McQuade. "How many rooms? One? Two?"

"Three."

"Oh?" Pity was evident in Felix's frown. "You're slipping, my friend."

"Yeah, well—" McQuade shrugged "—it happens. If things work out, it'll only be for a couple of nights."

Felix grinned. "That's right, McQuade. Think positive."

"Our stay. We'll be heading out after I make some arrangements with one of your many cousins." McQuade tossed some folded bills across the desk. "So what have you got?"

"I'll give you what I got left, McQuade. Two pretty nice rooms, one not too nice—you can make do." He palmed the bills with a thoughtful smile. "As for the cousin..."

"Just give me the keys. I'll explain later what kind of cousin I'm looking for."

Felix produced three keys from a drawer and handed two of them over. "Be a gentleman and give these to the ladies. You take this one." McQuade nodded, distributed the keys and shouldered his duffel bag. Felix closed the drawer and flashed another grin. "Don't worry, McQuade. I got all kinds of cousins."

Elizabeth opened the louvered doors and discovered that her room had a small balcony overlooking the sea. She filled her lungs with salty sea air and thought of home. The sand was a little whiter there, the sea a brighter shade of azure. De Colores was paradise, and she'd been cast out because she'd had a tryst with the devil. The minute she set foot on the sands of her home, she would be an outlaw, a fugitive in hiding. What messes we make of our lives, she thought. She watched a curling wave toss itself over the beach and remembered. Not my son's life, though, she promised herself. She would not let Tomás suffer for her mistakes.

She walked to the bed, opened her duffel bag and extracted the one dress she'd brought. Her mother had always insisted on a dress for dinner. The loose-fitting white cotton would be comfortable. There was no need to worry about what Felix Santiago's cousins would think of her clothes. As long as there was one among them with a sturdy fishing boat, Elizabeth refused to concern herself with what McQuade expected for his generous tips or the degree to which Santiago was anxious to accommodate him with cousins. As long as McQuade did his job...

There was a rap on the door accompanied by Ronnie's voice. "Elizabeth? Ready for dinner? McQuade's waiting."

Ronnie sat on the bed and watched Elizabeth fasten the straps of her sandals.

"I thought McQuade would be getting acquainted with one of the Santiago cousins by now," Elizabeth said, surprised to hear the catty tone in her voice. She quickly added, "Of course, part of his job is to make those contacts. We'll need help from these people."

"The only contact he's made so far is with me and Felix. We decided I'd leave for De Colores in the morning." Elizabeth sat up and was greeted by Ronnie's knowing smile. "He's planning on dinner with you. Said he wanted to return some favor and make sure you eat something, which we've both noticed you haven't done all day."

"I'm too excited." Elizabeth dismissed the idea of food with a wave of her hand. "You've made more plans already?"

"I'll be looking for you guys at that little village about half a mile from the airfield."

"El Gallo?"

"That's the one. There's a cantina there where we'll touch base, McQuade says. After he gets your son, I'll fly you guys out." Ronnie's blue eyes sparkled as she leaned back and happily offered encouragement. "Easy as pie."

They were nearly the same age, but Elizabeth felt the weight of difficult years on her as she envied Ronnie's optimism. Ronnie's strawberry-blond hair and petite figure seemed more suited to the cheerleaders Elizabeth had seen at American college football games than to a woman who piloted her own plane. The world could be Ronnie's for the taking, Elizabeth thought as she returned the smile. "Easy as apple pie."

"Why do I say that?" Ronnie wondered. "Pie isn't easy. I couldn't make a pie to save my life." She hopped off the bed and reached for Elizabeth's hand. "Come on, I'm starving. McQuade might want dinner with you, but he's getting us both."

* * *

McQuade had had his shower and his talk with Felix, and he was on his second drink when the woman on his mind walked through the door. Her black hair draped prettily over her smooth, tanned shoulders, and her eyes were magnetic. The shapeless dress she wore did nothing to disguise the fact that she was a polished jewel.

"I figured the three of us might find something to talk about if I tagged along," Ronnie said brightly.

McQuade snapped out of his trance. "Ronnie. Sure. That's what I had in mind." He grinned, gesturing toward the third chair at the table. "A strategy session."

"You've made a number of plans already, from what I understand." Elizabeth took a seat. "I know I promised to follow your instructions, but I'd like to be present when plans are discussed. My son's safety is at stake."

"Yeah, I know. So is yours and mine. I'm looking for a hit-and-run mission. I'm the hit, and Ronnie's the run." A dark-eyed waitress sidled up to McQuade, and he raised an eyebrow at Elizabeth. "White wine?"

She refused to be anticipated. "Rosé."

"And orange juice for the kid." He shrugged and added for Elizabeth's benefit, "That's what she drinks."

"You'll be grateful for my clear mind and sound judgment when I get you off De Colores safe and sound."

McQuade flashed Ronnie a thumbs-up, and they shared a laugh.

"Have you discussed cousins with Mr. Santiago yet?" Elizabeth asked. She didn't like this cocky soldier of fortune routine. Her son was at the other end of this so-called hit-and-run.

"He's out shaking the family tree. He'll get me what I need."

"He said he had all kinds of cousins," Ronnie recalled as she surveyed the menu. "Must be a big family."

"*Cousin* is a general term for all kinds of relationships here," Elizabeth explained. "It's the same with the villagers at home. It's hard to keep everybody straight, so they're all cousins."

"I hope you've got a few," McQuade said. Elizabeth cast him a questioning look, and he added, "A few relatives. Friends. Sympathizers. Anybody we could trust."

"Everyone is afraid of Guerrero. We'll be fortunate if no one knows me besides my great-aunt."

He had no idea what other family she might still have, or what friends had turned their backs on her. She held her chin up as she talked about what amounted to being cast adrift, and McQuade felt an uncomfortable pinching in his chest. When the waitress delivered their drinks, he was glad to be able to toss off a casual, "Thanks, honey. You do good work. Now, if you can find me a nice piece of beef, something real tender and juicy, I'll pay whatever price you ask."

The waitress's smile said she was anxious to accommodate him.

They had finished their meal when Felix brought another chair to the table and joined them. "My cousin Rico will take you and the lady fishing the day after tomorrow, McQuade. He will ask too much money, but you can reason with him."

The discussion of the boat didn't interest Elizabeth. So long as they had one, she didn't care how much the fisherman asked. Her attention strayed to the door of the kitchen, which the waitress had left open, and Elizabeth watched a woman turn from her sink full of dishes to a toddler at her feet. The woman dried her reddened hands on the white towel that was wrapped around her waist and bent to lift the child into her arms. She kissed his chubby cheeks, and he laughed and grabbed a fistful of her hair. Chattering to him, she disappeared to another part of the room, and then the kitchen door swung shut. Elizabeth felt a warm hand cover hers, and she turned to find that Ronnie had sensed her need. She let Ronnie see her gratitude, while the men talked of boats and the prospect of fair weather.

Rico Santiago's prosperity was evident in the size of his belly, but not in the condition of his mouth. He was missing his front teeth. Still, he grinned with pride as he showed off his fishing boat. "Everything up-to-date," he kept saying. "Engine works good, generator, icebox—everything A number one." Elizabeth noted that the paneling inside the cabin had recently been varnished, while McQuade turned a knob on the radio and got static. "Radio works sometimes," Rico admitted with a shrug. "Who needs it?"

"We won't be making any announcements," McQuade said. "When was the last time you put in to De Colores?"

"Last week."

"Any trouble?"

"Never no trouble." Rico grinned as he rubbed his belly absently. "I got lots of friends."

"Good for you. We'll be heading for a little cove on the south side of the island where there's—"

"No port," Rico finished, shaking his head. "Nothing but rocks."

"You can get us in close enough. We'll use an inflatable raft. And then, as far as any of your friends are concerned—" McQuade clapped a hand on Rico's shoulder and returned the smile "—you don't know anything about any Americans." He was promoting the assumption that Elizabeth was American, too.

"Ignorance can cost a great deal." The spaces in Rico's smile might have been filled with dollar signs as his eyes glistened with greed.

"You'll be well paid," Elizabeth assured him, and she turned to McQuade. "I'm pleased with the boat."

His scowl was enough to set her back a step. "You're easily pleased." He gestured toward the steps that led to the deck. "After you. Let's go out for a smoke, Rico, and talk this over. It's a wise woman who hires a man to do business for her."

"It's a wise woman who appreciates quality." Rico followed his prospective passengers as he sized them up mentally. He would be a hard sell, but she had the money.

"That's what I told her when I hired on." A fresh breeze greeted them on deck as McQuade shook two cigarettes out of a pack and offered Rico one. "We're paying two thousand just before our raft hits the water and another three when we've accomplished our mission and gotten back here." He expelled a lungful of smoke, and the breeze carried it away. "If we're picked up on that island, it won't speak well for somebody's ignorance."

Rico considered the wonderful American cigarette between his fingers and told himself that five thousand American dollars was a lot of money. Felix had said that McQuade didn't make mistakes. Rico had a good chance of getting the full amount. If not, even two thousand . . .

"McQuade!"

All three heads turned to watch Felix march purposefully over the pier's weathered planks. "McQuade, I have bad news," he shouted as he reached for the hand McQuade offered him. When he stood before them, he shaded his eyes against the sun and announced, "Miguel Hidalgo has been assassinated."

Chapter 3

The deal is off, McQuade."

McQuade stood his ground, hands on his hips, legs apart, as he braced himself against the easy rocking of the boat. "What do you mean, the deal's off?" he bellowed at Rico. "We haven't even got a deal yet." He tried to keep an eye out for Elizabeth, who was quietly separating herself from the group, as he turned to Felix. "Where'd you get this story about Hidalgo?"

"It was announced on the radio. Guerrero blames a rebel faction. He claims to have those responsible in his custody."

"Rebel faction, hell." McQuade shook his head. "Poor damn bastards'll be dead before the day's out, and Guerrero's home free." Elizabeth stepped off the boat and onto the pier, and McQuade scowled as he watched her shoulder her way past two men, narrowly missing a collision with a third. "Hey, lady, we've got a problem here," he shouted. She kept walking.

"De Colores is too damn hot now," Rico said. "With Guerrero in control, suspicion is enough to put a man away for good. I could lose my boat."

McQuade surveyed the deck. "What's it worth to you?"

Rico dragged a fishing net off the deck and busied himself with it, finally shaking his head. *"¡En absoluto!"* he mumbled. The sound of his own refusal brought new conviction. *"¡Ni de vainas! ¡Ni bamba!* Not for love or money, *señor."* He squeezed his eyes shut for a moment, then shook his head harder. "The money is good, but not that good."

"Could be better, huh?" McQuade laid a hand on the man's shoulder and waited until Rico looked him in the eye. "The greater the risk, the greater the reward. I could double that reward for you, Rico."

Rico sighed, still wagging his head as though he were dragging a ball and chain with it. "Maybe in another few weeks, after things cool down over there, but not now, McQuade. I got too much to lose." He gestured widely from where they stood on the port side of his boat toward the bow. "A boat like this? They would be waiting for the chance to confiscate it and give it to some fat colonel's mother-in-law."

McQuade knew when he had his man—and when he'd lost him. He turned away from Rico and caught a glimpse of Elizabeth, who was hurrying toward the beach. "Get me somebody else," McQuade told Felix as he stepped over a coil of rope. "Somebody who hasn't got so much to lose."

He vaulted over the side of the boat and hit his stride. As people saw him coming, they moved out of his way without comment. He broke into a jog and bounded down the wooden steps to the beach. When he caught up with her he slowed his easy, loose-limbed gait, and they left boats and fishermen behind them.

"There are a hundred other fishing boats around here that can make the trip," he told her as he fell into step beside her. The breeze carried her hair back from her face and flattened the neckline of her batiste top against the curve of her breast. He wanted to turn around and walk backward just so he could look at her. She seemed not to notice him, so he tried again. "All we have to do is find a fisherman who doesn't listen to the news. We'll find a ride to De Colores."

"I'm sure these people have reason to fear Guerrero, too." She walked faster, planting each step more firmly in the sand. "He spent time here while Miguel and the general prepared for the coup on De Colores. He was like the fighting cock who has to be restrained when he smells the arena. He couldn't be trusted not to—to jump the gun, as you say."

"Where were you then?" It was one question in a long list of them that he already wanted to put out of his mind. He'd seen enough of Guerrero to know that this woman didn't belong with him, and he needed to know how she'd gotten mixed up with that madman in the first place. Whenever he thought about it, the scenes he conjured up weren't the kind he liked imagining for her. He told himself not to get personal, not to anticipate any answers, but he did it anyway.

"I was on De Colores with my baby." She turned her eyes toward him, defying him to judge her, and she kept walking. "I was allowed to return home when my pregnancy became . . . burdensome. Before that, I followed him."

"By choice?"

"In the beginning, yes." With the admission, her pace slowed, and the stiffness went out of her shoulders. "It was my choice," she said almost inaudibly, then spun on her heel and faced the sea. "Poor De Colores. Miguel was your last hope."

McQuade thought he heard tears, but he found none when he looked at her face. He shoved his hands into his pockets and let his gaze follow hers out to sea. It was not the time to pry into her soul with his eyes.

"Miguel was a teacher, you know. We were both among the fortunate few who could afford to go to college." Edging closer to the water, Elizabeth allowed the tongue of the next wave to slosh over her sandals, and then she watched it retreat, pulling a collar of sand around her heels. It was a soothing feeling.

McQuade stood close behind her and waited for her to tell him more. He lit a cigarette for something to do in the meantime, thinking he was the closest thing she had to a friend right now, but that patience wasn't his long suit. He had found that whenever she gave him a scrap of herself, he devoured it and had to bite his tongue to keep from asking for another.

She stood there, letting the water slip over her feet as she reviewed her memories. Finally she took a step back and tossed her hair, letting the breeze carry it away from her face. "I was several years younger than Miguel, and by the time I was a freshman, he had finished graduate school and was teaching at the University of Massachusetts. He could have forgotten all about De Colores, except, perhaps, for a convenient place to vacation. But he brought his fine American education home and offered it to his people. Those with foresight loved him for it."

"And you?"

She smiled, remembering. "He was my first hero."

That was a scrap he could have done without. He didn't like hearing about the first, and he sure as hell wasn't going to ask about the second, who had somehow become her husband. "What about those who lacked foresight?" he wondered instead. "I take it they didn't appreciate his efforts."

"The former government saw no need to make students out of what had been cheap labor. There had always been some schooling for the younger children, but as they got older, they were needed in the cane fields, or on the fishing boats, or even in the market, to weave straw goods. Miguel dreamed of a high school education for every child."

"Can't argue with a dream like that," McQuade admitted, flicking his cigarette into the water. "I'd say go for it. Take over the government."

She didn't hear his sarcasm. When she turned to him, he knew she hadn't heard him at all. "They killed him for that," she whispered. "Guerrero killed him. For that dream and all the others."

Suddenly the pain of her loss filled her, and she was drowning in it. But she didn't cry. There was no room in her eyes for tears, and none in his mind for sarcasm. A man who thought he had no patience for tears stood waiting for them to come from a woman who refused to share them. He wanted her to lean against him, and he wanted to hold her. He reached for her even as he told himself not to. When she backed away, he looked down at his own empty hands and felt like a fool.

She held her head high, and her hair blew back from her face. "I mourn without falling to pieces, Mr. McQuade."

"Mr. McQuade" struck him like a dart. "I can see that." Raising his hands in quick surrender, he took his turn at backing away. "Don't let me interfere. God knows I'm no saint. For a minute there I just thought you might need a friend."

Elizabeth watched him head down the beach in the direction of the Oyster Shell. The waves soon ate up the tracks he'd left on the beach. His long legs scaled a sandy dune without breaking stride. He was an arrogant man, she told herself. He assumed too much—that she needed something from him, that she wanted to be touched by him. He disappeared over the incline, and she stood there watching the crest of the hill and listening to the sea.

* * *

Felix was a welcome sight. McQuade needed a man to talk to about the job he had to do. He needed to get his mind on a neat set of priorities—a boat, a clandestine drop-off, a chance to slip into the palace and snatch the kid, a rendezvous, an airlift. He wanted to start the images rolling around in his mind so he could make them click into place. Felix was bound to make more sense than Elizabeth Donnelly did. One minute she was practically serving McQuade breakfast in bed; the next she was pining over her ex-husband's political cohort but shrinking back from any expression of sympathy McQuade might have offered. Who could figure the woman? He joined Felix at the bar and ordered a drink.

"I got other cousins, McQuade." Felix tossed a book of matches across the bar. McQuade snatched it up and lit a cigarette.

"Braver than Rico?"

"Oh, sure," he said with a nonchalant gesture.

McQuade blew a quick stream of smoke past Felix's shoulder. "Show me one."

"Give me a few hours. I've got feelings out."

"Feelers." Felix gave him a confused look, and McQuade laughed. "You've got *feelers* out. And I sure as hell don't want to talk about *feelings*. I want to have a couple of drinks, talk man to man, blow a little smoke in your face and never once mention anybody's feelings." He took the drink out of the bartender's hand and tasted it. "No special recipe, right? Just bourbon and water?"

The young man nodded, looking to Felix for support. Felix waved him on his way and grinned at McQuade. "A man who comes to the islands with two women is asking for trouble."

"One left this morning, and she wasn't a woman, she was a pilot who happens to be female. The other one's a client who also happens to be female. So neither one of them is a *woman*, Felix, they're just—" he waved a hand in exasperation "—just female."

"The more dangerous sex of most species."

"Yeah. So let's not talk about them, either." McQuade settled the bargain by raising his glass. "Let's talk about cousins."

"Male or female?"

"Anybody you know who's got a boat," McQuade grumbled.

"And some measure of . . . guts?"

The two men grinned, man to man. "We're talking male equipment here, right, Felix?"

Laughing, Felix leaned toward McQuade and laid a hand on his shoulder. "Rico was a poor specimen. Without male equipment."

"Damn right. The hell with equal opportunity. Find me a *man* for this job, my friend."

They laughed together. "A man for business, and a woman for pleasure. It's sad to see Americans in such a state of confusion these days."

"Hemingway would've packed up all his gear and moved here permanently by now," McQuade decided. He drained his glass in silent tribute.

"Without question. And this was his favorite place to stay—this very place." Felix pointed to the floor and beamed.

When Felix beckoned one of his cousins to join them, McQuade offered to buy her a drink. Her name was Anita, and she softened and melted just the way McQuade figured a woman was supposed to do.

Elizabeth had walked for hours. The night was cool and calm. She'd watched one family clean the day's catch and joined another at their invitation for a fish fry on the beach. She'd refused all the while to think about Miguel's death or McQuade's assumptions. It always helped to lose herself among strangers. They could carry on with their lives around her, and she would be safe for the time she was among them. She could even pretend she belonged. But now it was time to go back.

There was a crowd at the Oyster Shell. She had intended to slip through the foyer and go upstairs without taking note of it, but she heard the rich sound of a familiar laugh, and it drew her inside. There was Sloan McQuade with, not one, but two women at his table. Neither one looked like a fisherman, and together they looked as though they could keep him up all night. The grin on his face made it apparent that such a prospect would be to his liking. That *was* her concern, she thought as she found herself headed for the table where the threesome was seated. She was paying this man well for his services.

"Come on and join us, princess! We're waitin' on one more cousin."

"I should think that two cousins would be company enough." It bothered her to see him with a drink and a cigarette in one hand and a woman's shoulder in the other. Her dignity would best be served by discussing business, she told herself. This cozy scene bothered her only because it might distract the man from doing his job. She stepped up to the table but ignored the chair he'd halfheartedly offered.

He shrugged. "If three's a crowd, four's a party. What're you drinking?"

"I'm not drinking anything, Mr. McQuade. Will we be able to get on with our business tomorrow?"

"I'm working on it right now, honey. Felix and me." Pulling his arm away from Anita, McQuade described a vague arc with his hand. "Felix is around here somewhere. We're putting our 'feelings' out." The expression struck him as funny again.

Elizabeth stiffened her back and braced herself against a rising tide of feelings of her own. "I'm not paying you to put out *anything*, Mr. McQuade. If you feel compelled to spread yourself around here, please come back and do it on your own time. We need a boat, and we need—"

"We need an understanding, Miss Donnelly." His back easily matched hers for stiffness as he set his drink down and crushed his cigarette in an ashtray. "You're paying for results, but you don't dictate the process. If you want to prance around here like a princess with a poker up her back, you go ahead. I don't have to feel friendly toward you to get the job done. But if I feel friendly toward anybody else—" he jabbed a finger in the air for emphasis "—you've got nothing to say about it, lady."

"Your so-called friendliness is of less interest to me than...than the time of day in Cincinnati! Make a public spectacle of yourself if you must, Mr. Mc-Quade, but get something done about this boat."

"Look who's making a public spectacle!" he shouted at her back as she walked away. "The island princess herself!" The surprised expression on Anita's face reminded him to settle down, keep it light. He came up with a conspiratorial grin. "The fancy barracuda."

Anita giggled and repeated, "Barracuda." Playfully punching his shoulder, she reminded him in Spanish that she didn't speak English. He realized then that *barracuda* was the first Spanish word he'd said since Elizabeth had walked in.

"Con permiso," he said. "Forgive my rudeness. The barracuda made me forget my manners." She'd made him forget that he'd been quite comfortably situated for the evening, too. He thought about whether to immediately press his advantage with Anita or hold off and light up another cigarette. He cursed himself as he busied his hands with a match. The best way to keep things light was to hang around lighthearted people. Anita had a ready smile for him. He checked to be sure, flashing her one of his own. "Another sangria?"

Yes, there it was, full of bright-eyed promise.

"Do you think we have time for another one, McQuade?"

He was waiting for Felix. Tipping his glass to his lips, he stared over the rim at the foyer and the stairway beyond it. She'd marched up those steps like she was right on time to meet the queen. God, she had nice calves. Especially for a barracuda.

"I have another name, you know. A first name."

Anita stroked his forearm. "May I call you by your first name?"

He'd heard it twice lately, but both times Elizabeth had ensnared him with it, pulled him in close with a single intimate word. Who the hell did she think she was, calling him Sloan and beckoning him with that doe-eyed look all the time, and then pulling away as though he had scales for skin?

"No, McQuade's good enough. Look, have another drink. How about you, Lila?"

"Lola," the other woman corrected as McQuade signaled the bartender.

"Nice name." Nice, hell, he told himself. If he'd been interested, he would have remembered it. And if that woman hadn't strutted in and interfered with his train of thought, he could have gotten interested. The drinks appeared, and he pushed his aside. His brain would have to soak up a lot of bourbon before it would let Lola or Anita replace Elizabeth in its tenacious cells. Damn the woman for spoiling his night.

"Enjoy your drinks, ladies. Here, you can flip a coin for mine." He dragged a handful of bills and change from the front pocket of his jeans and tossed it on the table. "I think I'll do me a little barracuda baiting before I go out and track Felix down," he muttered in English as his chair scraped across the floor.

Anita understood enough. The "barracuda" had gone upstairs, and McQuade's attention had been on those stairs ever since.

It was a surprise when Elizabeth admitted him to her room without putting him through any verbal indignities. She'd kicked off her sandals, and she'd obviously had to put some clothes on when he'd knocked, because he'd had to wait a minute for her to open the door. Her hair was wet, and she was wearing the same walking shorts with the same cotton top she'd had on earlier. There was one difference, and it caught McQuade's eye immediately. No bra. She closed the door and turned to him with an expectant look, which prompted him to ask his most pressing question.

"What the hell do you want from me, lady?"

Her chin shot up as she squared her shoulders and pierced him with a frown.

"Look, I'm sorry your boyfriend's dead. I liked him, too. He seemed like a good man. I was trying to—"

"He wasn't my boyfriend," she said evenly.

"Okay. Your hero, or whatever." He waved his hand toward the window as he recalled the scene on the beach. "I wanted to offer you a shoulder back there, just between friends. You weren't about to let me touch you, but you came unglued when you saw me with my arm around somebody else. What's with you?''

Elizabeth folded her arms over her chest. ''Your romantic activities don't concern me in the least. I came unglued, as you put it, because I saw that you'd been distracted from the job I'm paying you to do.''

''That won't wash, lady. You saw me sitting there with two women who obviously enjoyed my company, and you didn't like it.''

She turned away from him and took a moment to search for a reason. ''I was embarrassed for you.''

McQuade laughed. ''Embarrassed! Next to you, they were the best looking women in the house. I was doing okay.''

''Then go back to them, Mr. McQuade. I don't care whether you drink yourself into a blind stupor. It's a small island, so no matter where you find yourself when you wake up, you should be able to stumble back here, but I suggest you check your valuables at the desk before you go anywhere with those women.''

McQuade stared in disbelief. Had he left the price tag on the seat of his pants or something? ''Is that what you think I'm gonna do? Get rolled?''

''I'm sure that pair down there has gotten the best of better men than you.'' She tossed her wet hair behind one shoulder and settled her hand at her hip.

''No kidding?'' He wondered if she realized how increasingly transparent her blouse became with each wet spot her hair made. Was she posturing for him, or was she utterly absorbed in this asinine conversation? Intentionally or not, she was definitely turning him on. He took a step closer. "How can you be sure? How can you be sure better men than me even exist?"

"One can only hope. You came highly recommended, but I'm beginning to think my expectations were too high."

The soft curves of her breasts with the small, dark shadows of her nipples teased him from beneath the wet cotton, and when his subtle glance became a frankly appreciative stare, it was too late to cover herself. He'd already caught her in his arms.

"We expect to get what we pay for," he told her, ignoring her look of surprise as he lowered his head. "You're entitled."

He felt her resistance, but he closed his mind to it. He told himself that she fit against him too well to be less comfortable with it than he was. Her mouth was warm, and if she wouldn't move her lips against his, he'd coax them. He steadied her head with his hand, and he varied the pressure of his kiss, making a strong statement, gently asking a shy question, then pressing the issue again. He'd trapped her hands between them, and he felt her fists on his chest.

Like a willow, her slender frame bent, refusing to break under the strength of his embrace, but the rigidity was there. When he moved his hand along her spine and massaged the small of her back, he felt some of the tenseness melt away. Her lips responded then, just slightly, just enough to allow him to feather his tongue without their bounds. She relaxed her hands, and his chest expanded involuntarily as he sucked in the flowered scent of her.

God, she was sweet! He wove his fingers into her wet hair and kissed her hard, sliding his hand over her buttocks to press her tightly against him. He felt his breath catch, felt the fists form again. When he slid his kisses along the side of her neck, she drew a tremulous breath. Every muscle and tendon in his body hardened at the sound.

"I didn't ... I didn't mean it that way," she whispered.

Mean what? he thought. He was dimly aware that her voice had a strange edge to it, and he wanted to reassure her. He took her mouth again and kissed her, finding his way deep into her mouth and relishing the intimacy he found with her there. This was the way *he* meant it. He dragged his head away when her small whimper pierced his own fog of rapidly spiraling passion.

"I won't fight you," she said quietly, her chest heaving against his. "Just please ... don't hurt me."

He lifted his head to see her face. The fear that blazed in her eyes shook him to the core. It took him a moment to realize that his hand was tangled in her hair, and he opened it as he relaxed his embrace. "I'm sorry," he said and wondered where the sandpaper in his throat had come from. "Was I ... did I pull your—"

"No," she said quickly. "No, you didn't."

"I wouldn't hurt you, Elizabeth. You know that."

She nodded, but her eyes told him that she knew nothing of the kind.

He gave her some space, taking a moment to steady her on her feet. "Hey, look, I'm not forcing anything. That's not my style. But you've gotta admit—'' he adjusted the neckline of her blouse before he let her back away ''—*your* style's pretty provocative.''

She looked down and covered her chest with a trembling hand. ''It's wet,'' she whispered. ''I wasn't thinking.''

''So why start now?''

He stood there with his hands on his hips, making no attempt to conceal the physical effect she'd had on him. He figured she deserved the opportunity to be embarrassed for herself rather than on his behalf. He had nothing to be ashamed of. His was a man's response.

Elizabeth blushed and turned from him. ''I'm sorry. I overstepped my bounds.'' She glanced back. ''We both did.''

''I don't know what your bounds are, lady, but I know I didn't overstep any. I didn't do anything you didn't want me to do.''

''You flatter yourself,'' she said dully.

''Maybe.'' He took her chin in his hand and kissed her again, but it was over before she had time to raise her defenses. There was no battle—just a brief kiss. ''Yeah, you turn me on,'' he said quietly. ''But I can go back downstairs, and they'll have the same effect. So don't you flatter yourself, either.'' He started for the door, then hesitated and raised one finger of warning. ''Don't play games with me, Elizabeth. Because I'm not playing any with you.''

For long moments after she'd watched the door close behind him, Elizabeth stood in the middle of the room, her eyes fixed on the latch. She held on to herself, arms around her middle, waiting for the shaking to stop. It wasn't only the fear that had her trembling; it was the battle she'd waged to keep her arms from going around his neck. It was the way his kisses made her feel and the way she'd wanted to kiss him back. She'd been in control of her own life for a year now, and she didn't want that fragile state of affairs threatened. The old terror still held too much sway over her. She'd shown a woman's weakness when she'd promised not to fight him.

He'd said he wouldn't hurt her, and she wanted to believe that. Sloan McQuade was not Guerrero. And although he liked women, he'd made it clear he wasn't fussy, even if she did have a slight edge over the two ladies in the bar. If they were still downstairs, he was undoubtedly set for the night. She had to stay out of his private life. If she wasn't careful, she could end up actually caring what he did on his own time.

An hour later there was another knock at Elizabeth's door, and she leaped off the bed to answer it.

"It's McQuade."

His voice was a welcome sound, but she opened the door cautiously. He gave her a sheepish grin when she lapped a denim jacket around her chest. "I'm not looking for any more trouble, either," he promised, raising his right hand to attest to the fact. "I just thought you'd like to know—we've got a boat."

Chapter 4

Emilio Gomez had the face of a choirboy, but he was a working man. He had been a fisherman since he was five years old. Since his father's death, Emilio had had his own boat, which was small enough to be handled with the help of his seventeen-year-old wife and his thirteen-year-old brother. When Emilio introduced McQuade and the beautiful *señorita* to his family and his boat, *La Paloma*, his pride was as evident as Rico's had been in his fancier vessel.

Elizabeth glanced at McQuade as she extended a hand to Luisa Gomez. She hoped he realized that somehow they would have to persuade Emilio not to take his pregnant wife on the trip. It was expected that at thirteen a boy would do a man's work and take life's risks upon himself, but Elizabeth would not endanger this woman's unborn child.

McQuade put his hand on the young fisherman's shoulder ,and took him aside. Emilio was a head shorter than McQuade, but years of hauling nets had built muscle in his arms and chest. The two men were an artist's contrast as they stood together at the end of the pier, McQuade's golden head bent over Emilio's shock of straight black hair.

"You didn't tell me your wife was pregnant."

Emilio met McQuade's expression of concern with one of indignation. "You did not ask, *señor*. Why should it be of interest to you?"

"I told you there would be some risk involved. We're not welcome at De Colores. We won't be announcing our arrival to the officials at La Primavera."

"I understand that. But my wife goes with me—always."

McQuade reached for a cigarette and realized he was out of them. He hated scenes like this. Ordinarily he let people make their own decisions, just as he made his. The wife wanted to go along, and the husband knew the score. Fine. But there stood Elizabeth, sending him distress signals. She was worried about the baby. Okay, he didn't like it much himself, but these people had a life to live, too. On these islands, only the princesses like Elizabeth Donnelly took time off to be pregnant. Luisa Gomez would labor beside her husband until she labored with her child.

"How about if I put her up at the Oyster Shell?" McQuade suggested hopefully. "Give her a little vacation until you get back."

"My wife is a respectable woman. She does not stay at the Oyster Shell alone."

"Does she have a girlfriend who could stay with her?"

The idea was clearly repugnant to Emilio. "My wife does not stay at the Oyster Shell, *señor*."

McQuade gave Emilio an understanding pat on his bare shoulder. "I don't think this is going to work out, *amigo*, but I appreciate your position."

Luisa took two tentative steps toward McQuade. "We were going to De Colores anyway." Her husband gave her a sharp look, but she continued. "My sister lives there." Her smile was hopeful. "My sister is married to Emilio's brother. We visit often." Her hand went to her small, round stomach. "I have three months to go."

"Luisa!"

"Emilio, these people are worried about me!" She turned to Elizabeth. "There is no need to worry. You need a way to get to De Colores, and we are going there."

"Here, *amigo*." McQuade offered Emilio a thick wad of money. "Get your boat ready. I want to be on the island tomorrow night. Your wife is your business."

Elizabeth thanked the couple and preceded McQuade down the pier, offering him a sidelong glance when they stepped onto the sand.

He raised one eyebrow. "Your pilot, my fisherman."

Adrenaline gave him a heightened sense of personal power when he prepared for the final leg of a mission like this one. McQuade didn't see himself as a silver screen commando, but he did arm himself when the job required it, and he was proficient with all the weapons anyone could name. The 9mm semiautomatic pistol he was turning over in his hands as he sat on the edge of his bed fitted the bill for this job. He reached for the can of gun oil, the rag and the cleaning rod he'd set out on the nightstand.

He knew the real challenge lay in accomplishing his mission without firing a shot—getting in and out of a hot spot without anyone knowing about it until he was long gone. The exhilaration he felt after the slick, clean execution of a mission was what kept him coming back. He grinned at the sleek weapon that lay in his hand. That thrill and the money. There could be no better reason for...

"Mr. McQuade? May I speak with you for a minute?"

That thrill, the money, and a mother who wanted her kid back. "Come on in."

Elizabeth's eyes widened visibly when she stepped into McQuade's small room and saw the weapon in his hands. He waited for her reaction, and when it came— "Is that the biggest gun you have?"—he tipped his head back and enjoyed a hearty laugh.

She wasn't sure why he was laughing so hard. "What if you have to face something...something bigger?"

McQuade examined the pistol and worked hard to control his mirth. "Maybe you'd better tell me what Guerrero's got."

"He may have a missile by now for all I know."

McQuade sputtered, and Elizabeth smiled at the idea that he found her suggestion so entertaining. "He might have it pointed right at Washington," she added, thinking she was on some kind of a roll.

"Better at them than me." Forcibly straightening his face, McQuade held the pistol toward her. "This is not a gun, honey. This is a Browning Double Action Hi-Power. It's a semiautomatic pistol. Have you ever used one?" She shook her head. "Then give it a chance before you dismiss it for lack of size. I'm not going to get too far in La Primavera with a submachine gun hanging over my shoulder."

She stood beside him and looked down her nose at the weapon. "I hope you don't have to use it at all. I wondered if there was anything I should be doing— preparing. I need to...to *do* something."

McQuade patted the place next to him on the bed. She hesitated, and his eyes softened with boyish innocence. "Relax, Elizabeth. I swear I won't bite you. This is business. We're getting ready to do a job together. We're going to have to learn to trust each other, you know."

She sat down as though she weren't sure the bed would hold them both. "I know that. I don't know why I behaved the way I did last night." She sighed, tilted her head back and let her shoulders sag a little. "There was no excuse for the way I spoke to you downstairs. That was your business."

"Well, I know why I behaved the way I did, so I guess I'm one step ahead of you." His smile offered no censure, and the one she returned made him feel lighter inside. "Anxious to get this thing under way?" She nodded. "Kinda makes you feel itchy inside, doesn't it?"

"Maybe if I could help you—" she tipped a long, slender hand toward his lap "—polish your weapons?"

"This is it," he told her. "This and a little .38 Special that I thought might come in handy if you..." Her eyes widened. "And a hunting knife. Disappointed?" She shook her head quickly, and he laughed. He rubbed the rag over the pistol and laid it in her hands, watching her reaction. She stared at it as though he'd pulled the pin on a grenade and handed it to her. "You must have been around them before."

"I've lived with violent men," she said quietly. She'd expected it to be heavier. Its dull matte finish gave it the look of death, but the metal was warm from his hands. "But I've avoided their guns."

"There isn't much to it." He reached over to point out the mechanism. "You pull the trigger, it fires a bullet. Pull it again, it fires another one, just like Old Faithful. With the chamber loaded it'll deliver fifteen rounds before you have to change the clip to reload. This one has a pretty strong recoil, which takes some getting used to, but the .38 is smaller and doesn't have as much kick to it." He wrapped her hand around the butt of the pistol as though he were molding clay. "It's not loaded, Elizabeth. It can't hurt you. If you're going to insist on sticking your pretty little neck out, it wouldn't hurt for you to get comfortable with one of these."

"I could never be comfortable with it," she said. She touched the trigger with the tip of her index finger.

"You have to think of preventing harm to yourself. Nobody wants to think of killing somebody."

"I've thought of it." Her fingers curled around the crescent shape of the trigger. "Many times."

The idea was all the more chilling because it came from her. He sat very still, anticipating an explanation. Such delicate, clean hands were incongruous with the piece of steel she held in them. The breasts he knew were round, soft and fully feminine rose and fell on a heavy sigh as she studied the weapon. Then she handed it back to him, almost reluctantly.

"That's why I couldn't be comfortable with it." She looked up at him, and he felt himself drowning in the depths of her dark eyes. "You said I had to think about preventing harm to myself. But when I'm afraid, I *can't* think. I can only feel. I can only be afraid." She glanced away. "But later, after the fear goes away, then I start thinking. I think about having a gun like yours. I dream of having your courage, your confidence, your body."

McQuade swallowed hard and reminded himself that she hadn't really meant what she'd just said. After last night, though, he sure as hell wanted to have *her* body. But there was more to it than that. He had a queasy feeling now, born of the realization that she was telling him about someone else who'd wanted her body. Some man who'd shown her enough cruelty to make her wish him dead. Someone like Guerrero. He could deal with the bile rising within him as he guessed the source of Elizabeth's fear. McQuade would repay Guerrero. Harder to handle was the growing urge simply to shield her with his body and protect her from the world.

He searched for a remark to cover himself, and he found a cocky grin to go with it. "That's why you hired me, honey. Don't go wishing for a man's body. Yours is great just the way it is."

Elizabeth watched him stow his pistol in an aluminum frame backpack. She'd said too much. There was something about this man that made her reveal more about herself than she intended. It was just as well that he'd managed another of his one-dimensional male remarks, to remind her to get back to business.

"Are we in need of any kind of provisions?" she asked. "Perhaps I could go to the market."

"I've sent someone out with a grocery list." He set the backpack on the floor beside the bed, propped a pillow against the headboard and leaned back. "Mind if I have a cigarette?" She shook her head, and he struck a match. "It'll be hardtack, jerky and stolen bananas most of the time, so eat hearty tonight." He turned his head to send a stream of smoke toward the open window. "I'm going to ask you to make room in your pack."

"Of course. I wish I had one like yours." His hiker's backpack held a small sleeping bag and a foam pad tightly rolled and strapped to the bottom. He'd stashed his pistol in the nylon compartment in the middle, and there was a larger compartment on top with a couple of smaller pockets. She was sure that one was reserved for cigarettes.

"You do." McQuade hopped off the bed, stuck his cigarette in the corner of his mouth and pulled his big green duffel bag out of the closet. From it he produced another black nylon pack. "Smaller version for women. Think you can handle it? Here, try it on."

Elizabeth put her arms through the straps and watched him adjust them. "How thoughtful. I could have—"

"You hired an outfitter for this little trek, sweetheart. I come complete with brain as well as brawn." His eyes twinkled when he drew a laugh from her. "Looks great on you. Matches your hair. You'll have to carry the grub, since I'm totin' the guns," he drawled.

"That's fair." She slipped out of the nylon webbing and examined each zipper and buckle. "Where do you get these things? Army surplus?"

"You go to army surplus, you get weight and plenty of it. You want efficiency, you get into sporting goods. Those wheat germ lovers know how to take a hike." He took a long drag on his cigarette, then crushed it in

an ashtray on top of the bureau. A cloud of smoke
dissipated around his head while he dug into one of the
pockets of her backpack.

"Look at this." He came up with a handful of canvas that he unfurled with a flick of his wrist. He held
the child carrier toward her by the straps, and she set
the backpack on the floor to take a closer look at the
next gadget. "You can use it in front or in back, but
it leaves your hands free—*my* hands free. I expect to
be carrying him when we're on the run." He didn't
know what to make of the dazed look on her face.
"It's for Tomás," he offered, his voice gentling on the
name.

Elizabeth came to her feet slowly and reached for
the carrier. In what seemed like another lifetime she
remembered buying a tiny sleeper and imagining the
baby she would bring home from the hospital in it.
The sleeper had helped to make his imminent birth
really seem possible. She hadn't seen him for almost a
year now, but she would soon take him home in this
child carrier. The scrap of canvas somehow made that
a certainty. McQuade had provided something to carry
her son in. She looked into his eyes and warmed to his
reassuring smile. It made all the difference to know
that he, too, believed it would happen.

There was a knock at the door, and a woman spoke
Spanish through the crack she boldly provided for
herself.

"I brought the things you asked for, McQuade. Is
it safe to come in?"

They drew apart. Elizabeth turned her back on the door and rolled the canvas back up as McQuade let Anita in. She handed him a package, and he sorted through the contents.

"Good. You found that powdered stuff. And ... what's this?" He sniffed at something wrapped in paper. "Dried fish?"

"Smoked and dried. I do good work, don't I, McQuade?"

Elizabeth stiffened at the suggestiveness she heard in Anita's tone. She tucked the carrier into its pocket and held the backpack in her arms like a cradle board. "I'll go pack my things," she said.

"Not so fast, lady." McQuade rustled through his duffel bag again and came up with several handfuls of neatly wrapped plastic packages. Elizabeth stood holding her backpack, while he stuffed the middle pouch with provisions. "Food, first aid kit, batteries," he said, checking off items on a mental list.

"I think I've got an overgrown Boy Scout on my hands." Elizabeth took perverse pleasure in speaking English. She glanced at Anita to see if she felt sufficiently excluded.

She did. "*Tienes un cigarrillo,* McQuade?"

He offered a quick smile over his shoulder. "Sure. *Sí. Un momento.*" Turning back to Elizabeth, he asked, "Shall we have one more good meal together before we head out?"

"I've already asked to have something brought to my room." She wanted to invite him to join her, but Anita was holding fast to her station by the door, reminding Elizabeth that she would be waiting after he left Elizabeth, as she had no doubt been waiting the night before. "I know I should get as much sleep as I can."

"Yeah." His voice was flat. "It'll be a short night even if you can get to sleep." She nodded. He zipped the pouch and dropped his hands to his sides, asking her with his eyes to change her mind. When she didn't, he backed away and found his keep-it-light tone again. "Don't stuff that thing too full. I'll be knocking on your door when it's time."

As she walked down the hall, she heard Anita's sweetly intoned, *"Gracias."* Elizabeth hoped the woman would gag on McQuade's cigarette.

Much later, Elizabeth lay in bed and recanted every unkind thought she'd ever had toward Anita or anyone else. She forswore all bad habits and promised Tomás to the priesthood if only she would be allowed a few hours' sleep. She closed her eyes and tried to remember her baby, but she'd learned long ago to put him from her mind to save her sanity, and now she harbored a superstition against thinking about him too much. Fate had a way of holding something good out to her and then twisting it into something terrible just before she touched it. She mustn't let fate see the pinnacle of her hopes anymore. She must, she decided, shroud that pinnacle in mist and not even think of it herself.

But how bleak a life was without dreams! She closed her eyes and listened to the sea fling itself against the sand, hoping the sound would lull her to sleep. She pictured each wave, and soon she began to doze.

She felt cool water around her feet and warm sunshine at her back. She was sitting on a small dock, waiting for the man who was walking along the beach carrying a child in a sling strapped to his back. He waved, and she waved back. Sloan was bringing Tomás to her. Her heart swelled with joy when she recognized their smiling faces—both of them! Then a shadow fell across her own face. She turned as a man sat down beside her, and she saw the mark that identified him.

The scar was as red and angry as the eye it bracketed. Cold terror stilled the blood in her veins. He was talking to her, but she couldn't make out his words. His voice was the sound of gravel washing over sand. He jerked his chin toward Sloan and Tomás, waving his hand in their direction. And in his hand he held a deadly, dull black pistol. Elizabeth tried to reach out, but her arms wouldn't move. She tried to call out, but she had no voice. Horrified, she watched him take aim . . .

Elizabeth sat bolt upright, peering into the darkness. Her heart pounded wildly, and her whole body trembled. The walls were too close around her. She threw the sheet back and scrambled from the bed. The cotton shift she'd planned to leave behind came into her hand first. She pulled it on over her short nightgown and fled from the room on bare feet.

*   *   *

McQuade sat astride the wooden seat of a swing that hung from a big steel pipe frame on the stretch of beach belonging to the Oyster Shell. His habit of sleeping when he had nothing better to do wasn't helping him at all tonight. He'd had dinner and a couple of drinks with Anita, and then he'd sent her on her way. Things hadn't clicked with her, which was fine with McQuade. He was looking down the barrel of a high-energy situation, and he was feeling pretty good. Wait a minute—not *this* good. Not good enough to conjure up the moonlit mirage that had just glided into view.

His left hand slid down the swing's heavy chain. His right, holding a forgotten cigarette, was braced on his thigh. He sat perfectly still and watched her. Padding across the sand, she hurried toward the water as though it were her lover, her long hair wafting around her on the night breeze. The white dress he'd once thought shapeless hugged the front of her body and fluttered behind her. Luminous against the Caribbean sky, it suggested the shape of her breasts and the curve of her thighs.

This woman clicked with him. Her gears meshed with his and caused a humming in his head. God help him if this became a permanent hookup on his part; so far it was pretty damned one-sided. He helped himself to a lungful of smoke, thinking maybe it would pollute the whole works and break this crazy connection he'd come up with. He bent to bury the cigarette in the sand and came to his feet with the gears in his gut still shooting sparks to his brain.

"You can't sleep either, huh?" Her body jerked at the sound of his voice. He touched her shoulder as she turned quickly. "Sorry. I didn't mean to scare you."

A thick strand of hair blew across her mouth, and she brushed it back. "You move quietly, Mr. McQuade." She looked down and saw that his feet were bare, too. As she watched, the water washed over them and soaked the lower three inches of his jeans.

"I have a talent for sneaking around." He shoved his hands into his pockets just up to his knuckles. "Didn't Mike Romanov tell you that was one of my talents?"

She smiled, thinking of Mikal's description of this man. It hadn't begun to capture him. "Mikal thinks you have many positive attributes."

"And what do you think? Have you noticed any?" He didn't know what to make of that mystical smile, and she didn't give the affirmative answer he was hoping for. He shrugged off his disappointment. "Course, you have to hang out with me for a while before you get the full picture."

She turned her face back to the sea. "We'll be hanging out quite exclusively together for the next few days, won't we?"

"Looks that way. Unless I can talk you into staying here while I go get the boy."

"You can't." She swished her foot in the retreating water.

"Did you get any sleep?"

She shook her head. "Not the kind I wanted."

"You've got a lot on your mind." She nodded, pressing her lips tightly together. "Bad dreams?" he asked gently.

She wanted to tell him how bad. Perhaps in the dark of night, with the calm sea lapping at her, making her feel a little cleaner, she could tell him some of it. With the darkness around them, he wouldn't see the awful black scar her marriage had left on her.

"It's Guerrero, isn't it?"

"Yes." She was glad he'd said the name for her. She never liked to say it in the dark. "He's like a parasite under my skin. I scrub, and I scrub, but the taint remains. He haunts my sleep. Sometimes, when it's dark, I can even smell him."

McQuade's jaw tightened. His heart thudded against the walls of his chest, and he drew a long, deep, controlled breath. "What did he do to you, Elizabeth?"

"Don't ask me to tell you about those things. Let them be my secrets." *Don't ask me to put the worst part of myself on display for you.* She smiled up at him. "Let them be part of the mystery about me. Aren't men attracted to mysterious women?"

"Men are attracted to everything you've got, lady. The mysterious part is—" he shrugged, searching for the word "—worrisome. It keeps you bottled up and . . . and scared inside."

Best to keep ugliness in a sealed container, she thought, even if she had to serve as the vessel herself. "What's worrisome is what he might do to Tomás."

"Would he hurt a kid that young?"

"He's not above it, by any means. And, like most fathers, he wants a child who will follow in his footsteps." She gave a weary sigh and thought about that prospect for a moment. Then she said, "He would make a monster of my son."

"He won't get that chance."

There was a hard potency in his voice, and she tagged her hope to his power. A retreating wave dragged a large piece of coral along the side of her foot, and she bent to claim it.

"What kind of a family do you have?" she asked as she held her hand out. He took the coral and bounced it in his palm. "The regular all-American kind?" she wondered aloud.

"Not exactly. I had an old maid great-aunt who raised me. She died when I was twelve."

"What happened to your parents?"

"I don't remember my mother. When I was a baby she told Aunt Bertie she was going to look for my father, who'd split before I was born. We used to say she'd come back one day, but I don't think either of us really believed it." It was his turn to drift on a distant smile. "Aunt Bertie was a good ol' gal."

"What did you do after she died?"

"I lived in foster homes and boarding schools until I was old enough to join the marines. I was hell on wheels until that outfit got hold of me." He drew his arm back and pitched the coral at a cresting wave.

"Is that where you learned this trade you have now?"

"This trade?" He laughed. Sometimes he didn't know what to call it himself. "That's where it started. I was part of a Special Forces rescue team."

"Are you ... What would you call yourself? A detective?"

"I have a private investigator's license." He knew that was misleading. "I still call myself a specialist."

"Mikal Romanov called you the miracle worker. He said you've even found people who'd been declared dead."

McQuade chuckled. "Mike should talk. He's the one who makes miracles happen. He could talk the Hatfields into donating to the McCoys' scholarship fund."

"And he said *you* could recover the Golden Fleece. You should both go into advertising." They'd begun to walk, swishing their feet as the waves lapped gently at their ankles. "Did you ever try to find your mother yourself?" Elizabeth asked.

"Sure. But I'm my own worst client. That lady did not want to be found." A wave splashed high against his leg and spattered his T-shirt. He liked the feeling. "Either that, or she fell into the Amazon River and was eaten by piranhas."

"Maybe she tried to get back to you."

He shrugged. "I doubt it. Sometimes I like to imagine the piranhas."

"Oh, Sloan..."

"It isn't the same with you and your son." He stopped and touched her shoulder. "Believe me, it isn't."

"He offered no alternatives. If the hostages were to be released at all, I had to go with them. I had no choice." She lifted her hand to cover his. "Maybe she didn't want to leave you. Maybe she had no choice, either, Sloan."

He turned his palm to hers. "Tomás will know how hard you fought for him. If he ever doubts it, you just tell him to give McQuade a call."

"I'll do that." The promise came out as barely more than a whisper.

This is getting too heavy, he told himself, and he tugged at her hand. "Wanna swing? I'll give you a push."

They padded over the wet sand, then plunged across a dry stretch toward a stand of palms and McQuade's swing.

"Have a seat," he offered, gesturing with a flourish. The look she gave him said she wasn't sure she should do this, and he wondered how long it had been since she'd played at being a child. "Tomorrow I get serious," he told her. "Have some fun with me tonight."

She smoothed her skirt under her and sat carefully.

"Ready?"

"A *small* push."

"Got it." He pulled her back, saying, "This is my smallest push," and sent the swing on its first arc.

The wind took her breath away. On the second arc it took her cares away, and the years dropped away on the third. She pointed her toes and speared the night sky, loving the way her hair flew back. Her billowing skirt didn't concern her. Each time McQuade's strong hands sent the seat forward, she leaned back and stretched her long legs toward the stars.

"Higher?"

"Oh, yes!"

"How much higher?"

"As high as we can go!"

His laughter echoed hers. Her hips filled his hands, and he thought only a crazy man would push them away. He felt crazy, though, *good* and crazy.

"Oh, Sloan, it's not fair. I'm the one having all the fun!"

"I wouldn't say that."

"You have to take a turn. Let me push you."

It wasn't a bad thought, but he had a better one. He caught her high in the air and eased her to a stop. "We'll ride it double. Remember how that works?"

She hopped out of the swing with a smile that set her eyes aglow. "Show me."

He sat in the swing and indicated the margin of wood on either side of his hips. "Sit facing me and put your legs through here."

"Sit in your lap? Like this?" Suddenly trusting and without inhibition, she climbed on the swing and straddled him, deftly bunching her skirt in the V of her legs. "How do we get started?"

He took two steps backward and set them in motion. "Just rock with me."

"This way?"

"Mmm."

"I don't think we can get very high like this."

"Ohh, baby, I think you're dead wrong."

"Let's do it, then."

"Hang on."

They pumped until the chain went slack at the height of each arc. Elizabeth's breath caught high in her chest, and then she laughed. McQuade watched her lose herself in the free-flying feeling as he himself was lost in the sweet torture that was centered in the fulcrum they made together. She leaned forward, the wind at her back, and she saw the pleasure in his eyes. It was a pleasure she shared. He raised his chin, she lowered hers, and they kissed just as a wave lapped the beach not far away. Cool and wet became warm when he touched his tongue to hers, and when he drew it back slowly over the roof of her mouth. The swing slowed, swayed, and finally stopped, but the undulating sensation lingered where their bodies met.

"Elizabeth? That was one hell of a nice ride."

Chapter 5

La Paloma skimmed over the smooth-rolling sea like a song. The sun was high, and it scattered white sparkles over the surface of the water. Emilio hadn't been able to resist doing a little trolling on such a fine day, and they'd made a nice catch. McQuade was glad to lend a hand to keep busy, but it surprised him that Elizabeth had joined in, too. He'd watched her toss slippery fish around like an old salt and wondered if Emilio noticed the way Elizabeth had made a point to move Luisa aside and take over for her when the nets were hauled over the side.

Luisa used her time below decks to make the noon meal more special. It was a wonderful blend of Mexican and island flavors—spicy panfried fish, rice, corn bread, and fried plantains with rum sauce. Thinking

of the leathery-looking dried fish he might have to resort to within the next few days, McQuade had eaten
his fill. Now, content, he lounged in a folding chair,
enjoyed a cigarette and watched Luisa and Elizabeth
emerge, one after the other, from below decks.

Emilio was tending to his nets, but he looked up
from his work and smiled when he saw his wife.
McQuade looked from one to the other and was
touched by the pride they obviously shared in the
coming baby. Together they would become three.
Luisa turned to Elizabeth and whispered something.
They glanced at each other and giggled. McQuade
imagined Elizabeth as she must have appeared with the
same small round belly, and a warm feeling for her
spread though his own.

He beckoned her with a glance as he left his chair
and stepped up to the boat's railing. She came to stand
beside him, and he turned his back to the sea, braced
both arms behind him, closed one eye and grinned at
the sky. "Wouldn't this be the life? Sun and sea every
day. Fantastic."

"If it could be like this every day, then this would
indeed be the life." She smiled at the way the sun
glinted in his hair like a wealth of copper pennies. He
wore a dark blue short-sleeved shirt, jeans and blue
running shoes, and she thought he should have been
grilling steaks on a patio in some suburb of Miami.

"It's like this today, and this is it for me. My day as
a Caribbean fisherman. I love it." He gestured broadly
toward the couple at the bow of the boat. "Look at

Emilio. The sea is his home. He's got his wife by his side. Who cares about the price of fish?''

"Whatever it is, they work hard for it. And for Luisa, it can only get harder."

His face became sober as he pursed his lips and nodded. "That's true. Men get off easy when it comes to having babies." He turned to her, curious. "How did you do?"

The question took her off guard. "Do? I did all right, I guess."

"I mean, you know...was it hard?"

He seemed genuinely interested, even concerned, and she wondered whether Luisa's condition suddenly bothered him. She found herself smiling to reassure him. "No matter how hard the pain is, it's forgotten the minute you take your baby in your arms. Your getting off easy has its drawbacks."

Emilio raised his voice to Luisa just then, and McQuade jerked his head around and straightened his back, scowling. Luisa had stumbled over some rope. As he caught her, Emilio scolded her for being clumsy.

Elizabeth touched McQuade's shoulder. "He worries, too," she said quietly. Unaware of his audience, Emilio covered his wife's abdomen with his strong brown hand, and Luisa's face became as radiant as the sun above her head.

"If I ever have a baby, I won't miss a thing," McQuade mumbled as he watched the young couple. "I'll be right there the whole time." He felt Elizabeth's stare. His face got hot, and he knew he was treating her to a rare sight. Sloan McQuade was blushing.

Damn it, McQuade, you might as well look her straight in the eye and get it over with. You just blew yourself right out of the water.

She was smiling.

"It's gotta be—" he shrugged, searching for a word—*any* word "—fascinating as hell."

"And then some."

Shaking his head, McQuade turned to lean his forearms on the railing and face the sea. He couldn't restrain a self-conscious grin. Elizabeth laid her hand on his shoulder and leaned close to his reddened ear. "I never know what to expect from you," she said.

He laughed. "Lately, neither do I."

"Disarmed, you're completely disarming." He cast her a sidelong glance, his gray eyes sparkling. "Really," she assured him.

"Hell, I oughta just deep-six the Browning and the .38 Special, then. I'll be so disarming I won't need them. What with your big brown eyes, this pregnant woman, and your kid waiting in La Primavera, you guys have all my weaknesses covered."

She lifted an eyebrow, incredulous. "What about the bourbon, the cigarettes, the steaks and…what else was there?"

He knew he'd probably said "broads" if he'd run down the usual list for her. "I can buy all that stuff, remember?"

"Oh, yes." Her tone stiffened, along with the expression on her face. "Money."

He looked straight ahead at the blue-on-blue horizon. His blush had gone the way of her smile. "Yeah. That was it."

They stood together in silence for a time, and then Elizabeth decided to try another subject. "I know a place on the south side of the island where we could hide."

"Where?"

"Southeast. We'd put in at the cliffs above El Gallo."

McQuade remembered where the little village was situated, cane fields to the north and, at its back, a mountainous region thick with tropical vegetation. "On the southeast end? That's sheer rock face."

"I know a way up to the top," she told him. "I explored a lot as a child. There's an old pirate lookout point up there, the ruins of a tower. What's left of it is overgrown—"

"And probably home for hundreds of slithery critters."

"Then we'll ask them to vacate." She folded her arms across her chest and gave him a look that challenged him to match her nerve.

"You sure you remember the way up? I've got goggles that'll improve our night vision, but we'd be in deep trouble if you couldn't locate the trail."

"I know exactly where it is," she assured him.

With Luisa at the helm, *La Paloma* hovered as close as it could to the rocky beach, while Emilio and his brother tethered the rubber raft alongside and handed

McQuade's gear down to him. They lowered Elizabeth into his hands last, and with genuine concern for their safety, Emilio commended them both to God's care.

It was a moonless night, which McQuade counted as their first blessing, and they paddled the raft toward a rock formation high on the cliff that Elizabeth used as her landmark. There was little talk between them as they made their way toward shore, the hour approaching midnight. Waves splashed against the rocks as they slogged through the shallows in their running shoes, which protected their feet from the coral. When Elizabeth stumbled and scraped her leg, she was grateful for her soggy jeans.

McQuade let the air out of the raft once they were ashore, and then he made a tight bundle of the rubber and tied it to his backpack. No trace of their arrival could be discovered on the beach.

Elizabeth had no trouble finding the trail. They scrambled over a rocky incline and squeezed through some places that had once been easy passages for a child to negotiate. Behind what appeared to be solid rock was a rocky path that she remembered as a young girl's dream for climbing. Using hands and feet, they were soon on their way up the mountain.

McQuade had to hand it to her; she was as agile as a ten-year-old on the steep, rocky path. At the top there were trees growing thick and lush. They disturbed them as little as possible as they picked their way through the bushes until, shrouded in a dense copse of banyan trees, Elizabeth rediscovered her secret pirate hideout.

One set of stone steps led the way to a pile of rubble surrounded by a crumbling circular wall. There was no promise of shelter at first glance, but Elizabeth picked her way through the rocks and found another set of stone steps. "There's an underground room here," she whispered. In the dead of night it seemed inappropriate to raise her voice in this place.

McQuade lowered his backpack to the ground and removed the revolver and a handful of cartridges. He loaded it, rolled the cylinder into place and reached for the flashlight he carried in a sheath on his belt next to the knife. "Wanna place any bets?" he asked on his way down the steps.

"My money's already on you," she reminded him.

The passageway to what once must have been a storage room smelled like rich, dank humus. McQuade heard something rustling in the larger room ahead, and he approached with his back to the wall. He flashed his light from corner to corner and flushed out an iguana, which scurried over his foot and out the door. Feeling a little jumpier, he did another survey. Cobwebs were abundant in the room, which seemed to have been carved out of rock. A small pile of rocks stood in the corner.

McQuade felt more than heard the presence at his back, and in an instant Elizabeth was squinting into the beam of the flashlight. McQuade lowered the barrel of the .38 and sagged against the wall.

"Don't ever sneak up on me like that, Elizabeth. Not when I've got a loaded revolver in my hand."

"I'm sorry. I called, and you didn't answer."

"I didn't hear you."

"I didn't exactly *call*. I sort of hissed."

He groaned. "I could have mistaken you for a snake and shot you."

"Then you would only have gotten my foot. What did you find?"

He turned the light back on the room. "A hole."

"Oh, look! My gold!" She stepped into the light and pointed toward the rocks. "It's still here, right where I hid it."

"Great. Let's blow this joint and buy the island, lock, stock and baby."

"Scared?" It was a question she always asked sympathetically.

"Hell, no. This is perfect. Real cozy once we get rid of the wildlife." With his flashlight he took a swipe at a drift of cobwebs. "You actually came here to *play*?"

"I came here to hide my treasure," she said lightly as she slapped more cobwebs down.

"If you were young enough to be hiding treasure, you were too young to be up here alone."

"Probably. I'll go get your backpack."

He handed her the flashlight. "I'll get it. Remember, no lights outside."

The instant he was out of sight, she stopped breathing, and she couldn't draw breath until he returned.

"Turn it out of my face, honey."

"I'm sorry."

Her voice was thin and tremulous. It would have been unfair to taunt her with "Scared?" The place gave him the willies, but she was battling with something much deeper. He offered his hand, and she grabbed it and held on tight.

"It hasn't always been like this for you, has it?"

"No." She took a deep breath and exhaled slowly. "I'm fine. I just don't like being alone in a place like this."

"Hell, neither do I. Who would?" When she was done with his hand, he thought, he would set his backpack down. He wondered if she had any blood left in her fingers.

"I used to play alone all the time—eat alone, study alone. I've become such a baby." She sighed. "At night, sometimes I have to leave my bed and go outside."

"I hope you won't do that here. If you get the urge, let me know."

"Sometimes . . . I'm afraid I'll suffocate."

It was such a quiet confession that he had to strain to hear it. "If you feel like that during the night, wake me up. We'll go outside together."

She released her hold on him slowly. "How many flashlights do we have?"

"Two. And power to spare."

"Then I'll keep one close by."

McQuade opened the deflated rubber raft and spread it down as a mat. Elizabeth set about making her bed. As long as she knew he was there, she was all right. She decided they needed conversation. "I guess what you've been calling me isn't far from the truth."

"What's that?"

"Island princess. My grandmother had a plantation west of here, and I spent a lot of time exploring in these hills and along the beaches."

"She still there?"

"No. She died, and my father sold most of the land. The money I got from my mother was put in trust before my grandmother's death, though, and my father had nothing to say about it. We still had a house, but Guerrero laid claim to that."

"Along with everything else," McQuade added. "I've got one question."

"Hmm?"

"Where do you want me to sleep?"

"Right next to me." She gestured toward the spot, then looked up at him, quietly adding, "If you wouldn't mind."

"Mind? You kidding?" He unrolled his foam pad and lined it up next to hers. "I just had a thirty-inch lizard run over my foot."

Moments later she stiffened when she heard him start to unzip his jeans. She turned reflexively, and his hands stilled. "Look, my pants are wet, Elizabeth. Now, you can watch, or you can face the other way."

She did a quick about-face, then realized hers were wet, too. She flicked at the snap. "Are *you* looking the other way?"

"Hey, *I* gave *you* a choice." He laughed and then said with a gentlemanly drawl, "My eyes are averted, Miss Elizabeth."

Shucking her jeans with all the awkwardness of someone in too much of a hurry, she muttered, "I don't know if I can trust you quite this far, Sloan McQuade. You and all your weaknesses. I just can't be sure...."

She refused to look at him until she'd scooted into her sleeping bag and covered up. Then she risked a glance. Naturally he was smiling.

"You said you wouldn't look."

"I said my eyes were averted, honey. They were."

"How much did you see?"

"Not as much as I wanted to."

"Boorish American. I should have—"

"Can we turn off the flashlight?"

"Certainly. You can smirk in the dark."

She lay there in darkness for several moments listening to his breathing, concentrating on an awareness of his presence. It wasn't enough.

"Sloan?"

"Hmm?"

"Do you think we could touch somehow?"

"Touch...each other?"

"Shoulders or...or hands."

He sighed, muttering, "All my trials...come over here, princess. Lift up a little. Put your head on my shoulder. Better now?"

"Yes. Are you comfortable?"

Comfortable? Was she kidding? "Sure. You'll be okay. Just picture a nice sunny day. A bright sun-shiny field full of . . . full of grazing horses. You like horses?" She nodded against his chest. "Lots of sun, lots of flowers. Mares and their colts. Can you see all that?"

"Mmm-hmm."

"Good. You go to sleep thinking sunshine and flowers and horses in the field." He kissed the top of her head and closed his eyes. *While I lie awake feeling sorry for the poor jerk in the stud barn.*

"No!"

McQuade shot up. The pistol came into his hand immediately, and he stared into the darkness for an instant before it came to him that the voice was Eliz-abeth's. Easing himself back on his elbow, he ex-changed the pistol for the flashlight, aiming it at the wall above their heads. He leaned over her, but when he touched her, she tried to push him away.

"No, no. No más, por favor," she mumbled, whimpering like a child in pain.

"No more what? You're dreaming, honey." He touched her cheek and then drew her into his arms, gently rendering her struggling useless. "It's Sloan. Wake up, Elizabeth. Look at me. It's Sloan."

"No más." She groaned, pushing against his chest.

"I won't hurt you, baby," he whispered and pressed his lips against her forehead. "I could never hurt you. You're okay now. You're with me."

"Sloan?"

"Yeah." He leaned back so she could see his face.

She saw gray eyes instead of dark fury, golden hair rather than black, caring rather than cruelty. With two trembling fingers she touched his lips to be sure they were real. She closed her eyes, grateful for the solid feel of him.

"Oh, Sloan, you must think I'm loco."

"I think you're scared."

She sighed. "He won't let me sleep."

"How can I help?" He traced his thumb along her jaw. "What can I do for you, honey?" She stared at him. "We could zip the sleeping bags together."

"No."

"If I just held you . . ."

She was out of her bed and lunging for the door before he could protest.

"You sure you wanna go out there like that?" She froze. "Catch." He reached for the jeans she'd draped over her backpack and tossed them to her. "You stay by those steps till I get there," he warned as she faded into the dark passageway.

McQuade pulled his jeans on, tucked the pistol in the back of his waistband and reached for his backpack. "I need a cigarette. Look at me," he said in disgust. "I'm talking to myself." He stuck the end of the cigarette between his lips mumbling, "Maybe I'm the one who's loco."

Smoke curled around his head as McQuade fanned the match and pocketed it. Elizabeth was sitting on the low stone wall, and he joined her there. "I wasn't looking to compromise your innocence when I suggested—"

"I have no innocence to compromise." She took the cigarette from his hand, and he watched while she puffed on it with the ease of a lifelong smoker.

She handed it back to him, and he chuckled. "Is that the clincher? Would it corrupt you further if I offered you a whole one?"

"No, thank you. I stopped smoking when I became pregnant. I stopped being innocent long before that."

"What are you supposed to be guilty of?"

Hooking her bare foot over her knees, she brushed a troublesome pebble off her sole. "The original sin. I know too much."

He studied the perfection of her profile, the soft curve of her hair as it lay against her cheekbone, and the guarded look in her eyes. "You sure as hell couldn't prove it by me."

"And what do you know, Sloan McQuade?" She turned to him, squaring her shoulders. "What have you seen in all your travels?"

"I know loneliness." He lifted his shoulder invitingly. "I know what it's like when you need to be close to somebody."

Lowering her foot to the ground, she yielded to him, but didn't move any closer. "You talk like a woman sometimes."

"Don't knock it. Some of my best friends have been women." He took a quick, hard pull on the cigarette and spat out the smoke. "So how do men usually talk?"

"Without sympathy. They use vulgarity instead."

"Would you prefer that?"

"I would understand it better."

"Okay, I'll put it to you this way." He turned, bracing his hand on his thigh. "I wasn't looking to get laid back there, although if you'd offered, I sure as hell wouldn't have turned you down. You were scared, and I wanted you to settle down so I could get some sleep. And if you're so damn worldly, how come I feel like Jack the Ripper every time I put my hands on you?"

Elizabeth's eyes narrowed as she nodded. "That's more like it, Mr. McQuade. That sounded very masculine."

If there had been more light in the sky, they would have seen the light in each other's eyes and then the dawning of smiles. As it was, a duet of laughter broke the ice, and McQuade flicked his cigarette into a pile of rocks.

"So how should I talk around you, Miss Worldly Wise?"

"It might as well be your way, Mr. Macho. I'll expect the unexpected."

"Good." He sobered, catching her cheek in his palm, and her laughter faded, too. "Here comes the unexpected."

Their kiss was sweetly serendipitous. Elizabeth took one deep breath and leaned closer. The unexpected was supremely gentle. For all she'd come to know about men, she knew little of this. His arms were comforting. His strength posed no threat. He took her breath only after she'd used it, and he traded it for his. For all her experience, she hadn't known a kiss like his. It was an offer, not a demand. It was a sip of fine wine, a whiff of its bouquet. She tipped her head back and sampled, rolling the taste of him over her tongue and finding it to be smooth and wonderfully full-bodied. How dangerous would it be to ask him to fill her glass?

But that was not offered. When he drew back he suggested simply, "I want to hold you through the night, Elizabeth."

She smiled. There was such softness in his eyes, and that, too, was unexpected. "Will you tell me more about the horses in the pasture?"

Elizabeth had purchased a full cotton skirt and a loose blouse in Arco Iris. She had fastened her hair in a bun at the nape of her neck, and she hoped to find a broad-brimmed straw hat in the village. McQuade was an all-American tourist, from his loose-fitting shirt to his blue jeans. Only the pistol tucked in his pants under his shirttail spoiled the image. They walked into El Gallo without causing much of a stir.

McQuade knew most of the cantinas in De Colores, and La Gallina was one of his favorites. Antonio was a friend. And then there was his hot-blooded daughter, Chi Chi. As he held the door for Elizabeth, McQuade hoped that, with any luck, Chi Chi had forgotten him.

"McQuade! Man of my dreams! Ohhhh..." The dark young woman with the cherubic face lowered her outstretched arms, frowning. "You brought another woman?"

"I have another woman, yes. And you were going to get married to—what was his name?"

"Carl, I think. He was going to take me to Miami."

"Always Miami." Antonio appeared from the back room, offering a handshake. "McQuade! Our troubled island has seen little of you this past year."

McQuade took a seat at one of the cantina's three tables and pulled a chair out for Elizabeth as an apparent afterthought. They'd agreed that she would be a silent shadow during this visit.

"I've got some errands to run for the Red Cross, plus a little private investigating for a client back home."

Antonio dragged a chair close to McQuade and prepared to be included in his friend's wonderful secret dealings. Antonio loved American television, especially the detectives shows, and McQuade's visits were the highlights of any season. He flashed a conspiratorial grin. "What can I do for you, *amigo*?"

The question came as a surprise. "Nobody's been here looking for me? A woman named Ronnie Harper?"

"Another woman?" Antonio winked broadly. "I envy you, McQuade. They can't resist a man of action."

Antonio was one of McQuade's most reliable sources, but he wished the man would just answer his questions. He caught an icy glance from Elizabeth.

"The woman's a pilot, Antonio. She brings in supplies for the Red Cross. She was supposed to leave a message here for me."

"A message?" Antonio's eyes brightened as though the word suggested a gourmet delight.

"She's kinda cute," McQuade offered. "Boyish dresser. Reddish blond hair. She should've been here in the last couple of days."

Chi Chi piped up from behind the bar. "Doesn't sound like your type, McQuade."

"Has the woman been here, Chi Chi?" Antonio demanded. "You're not to handle McQuade's messages. That's *my* business."

"There have been no Anglos here for months, Papa. If one had set foot in the village, we would have heard about it."

The fact that the news disturbed McQuade also disturbed Antonio. "This secret message is for your client, no?"

McQuade was studying a pair of initials carved in the table. Ronnie had seemed pretty straight to him. Either he'd had her pegged wrong, or she was in trouble. He would have to do some checking, and that would take time—time he hadn't allotted in his plan.

"Ronnie Harper was my ticket out of here, Antonio. Can you find out for me if she was here? She island-hops in a Cessna."

"Security is getting tighter," Antonio said. "Since Colonel Hidalgo was killed, the police question every move anybody makes."

"Who do you think killed him?"

Antonio shrugged. "The government questions us, but we don't question the government." He leaned closer. "I think Guerrero worried about Hidalgo's popularity. But Guerrero says it was the CIA."

McQuade figured the CIA would have to double its forces to manage all the activity they were credited with, even the likely stuff—which this certainly wasn't. "Listen, Antonio, I need some information about Guerrero's kid. My client wants to know where he is, who's taking care of him, whether he's eating his vegetables—stuff like that. Who might know?"

Antonio glanced at Elizabeth and then flashed McQuade a grin. "That's easy, *amigo*. A girl from this village cleans the house where the boy stays. He's not at the palace. He stays with an old lady."

"Maria Adelfa?"

Both men turned to Elizabeth. "Yes, that's the one," Antonio said. Elizabeth nodded and quietly returned her attention to her hands, which were folded in her lap. "You can talk to the girl," Antonio offered. "She's Chi Chi's friend, but quiet as a mouse. You can trust her."

"You'll arrange that for me?" Antonio nodded vigorously, and McQuade laid a hand on the man's shoulder. "I trust you like a brother, Antonio. You're my eyes and ears in De Colores—you know that."

Antonio beamed. "And I'm undercover this trip. Not a word to anyone about this woman or me."

"Of course not. You hear that, Chi Chi?"

"Keep your voice down, Papa, or the whole village will hear." She leaned over the bar, her arms forming a frame to enhance the deep cleavage in her full bustline. "I don't want nothing bad to happen to McQuade."

"Then how about serving up some dinner?" McQuade suggested. "I'm fading fast."

By the time they left the village, McQuade had learned that Ronnie Harper's Cessna had hardly been on the island long enough to refuel. It didn't make sense to him; if she'd planned to skip out on them, why had she flown into De Colores at all?

His ace in the hole was Emilio, who had arrived at his brother's house that morning. Antonio had brought Emilio to the cantina and left the two men to talk privately. He had also arranged for a meeting with Juanita, the nurse's housekeeper. Things were falling into place nicely.

As they hiked through the underbrush toward their mountain retreat, McQuade figured he faced two major problems. One, the barometer had dropped suddenly, and he felt the heavy stillness of a tropical storm in the air. Two, he faced another night in close quarters with Elizabeth.

Chapter 6

The sky had lost its color. It appeared above the trees in eerie patches, neither gray nor blue, as though watercolors had run together in a painting and gotten muddled. Elizabeth knew the signs. Islanders accepted the warning as a matter of course, and they prepared themselves and their property as best they could. She knew better than to begrudge nature her timing, but the bitterness that rose in her breast as she neared the top of the mountain could not be reasoned away. It couldn't happen now. No power on earth should be allowed to stand in her way now that she'd come this far.

"If this blows over, I'm going to go in after Tomás tomorrow," McQuade told her. They reached a small clearing, and he stopped to take another survey. "Feels like this could get pretty serious, though."

"Why couldn't we go now, tonight?"

She looked hard, determined and dangerously emotional. She avoided looking up at the sky, although he knew she sensed the ominous signs as intensely as he did. They were in for one hell of a storm.

"I figure that I can make the slickest snatch at siesta time. Juanita's willing to help for a small fee." He raised an eyebrow her way. "And you aren't going anywhere near that house, so don't get any ideas. You'll be waiting on Emilio's boat."

"What if this doesn't blow over?"

"Then we wait it out."

"And what if—"

He took hold of her arm. "Don't give me any what-ifs at this stage, Elizabeth. You and I both know that if this island gets hit with a real hurricane, it'll be a whole new ball game."

"You'll back out?" she accused, pulling away.

"Hell, no, I won't back out. You think I'm..." Furious, he started up the hill again.

When he felt her walking close by his shoulder, he began calmly. "You learn to adapt in this business. You count on your own wits, not your plans, and you don't waste time worrying about the things you can't control." He glanced at her to see if he was making any impression, but he couldn't tell. She was staring ahead with a resigned, vacant look in her eyes. "Life is full of variables, Elizabeth, and the weather is one of them. But we're going to deal with that."

Her look told him that *she* certainly would. He decided to go over everything with her that night. If he laid it all out for her, it might boost her confidence in him. This was turning out to be the stickiest job he'd ever taken, and it was beginning to make him feel a little edgy. It wasn't the risk; he'd gone into the backyards of adversaries who were better trained than Guerrero's little army and far better supplied. It wasn't changing plans, and it wasn't the weather.

He knew damn well it was his client who was making him nervous, not his opposition. When somebody paid him fifty thousand dollars to do a job, that was usually all he needed as a vote of confidence. So why did he worry about this woman every time she got that look in her eyes? It was a complicated look, and he liked to keep things simple. Whether for a client or a bed partner, he liked to think he supplied a service and got what he wanted in return. He'd gone through thirty-six years that way, and he'd counted on sailing through at least another thirty-six with the same no-strings philosophy. And then along had come Elizabeth Donnelly.

They stopped to wash themselves in a mountain stream, giving each other the space they needed mentally as well as physically. Then they climbed to the top of the cliffs overlooking the sea, but neither of them made a prediction about what might come next. The threatening sky hung low over white-capped, slate-colored waters, making clear what was about to happen. The wind was picking up. Now was the time, Elizabeth told herself. Just before the storm hit. If she couldn't get back up here, she could find another place to hide with her baby, and no one would be able to search for her.

"I love to watch a storm brew," McQuade said absently. "The power grows right before your eyes." He shoved his hands into his pockets as he turned to her. "We should be okay down in the hole. The water should run out the side of the stairwell and down the hill." She nodded. "Storms bother you, too?" he asked gently.

"This kind of storm kills people," she reminded him. Her hair blew across her face, and she pushed it aside. "Yes, they bother me. I don't enjoy watching them brew." She walked away from him, her full skirt hugging her buttocks and the backs of her legs as it billowed out in front of her. Her hair flew forward, looking like the long leaves of the palms that bent above her in the wind.

"You're not going inside yet, are you? No telling how long we'll be stuck down there."

"I'm going to take the canteens and fill them in the stream," she shouted back.

He turned to the sea again and let the wind blow in his face. As he watched the storm clouds roll in, he realized that he was bothered by the way she had shouted at him without turning around. He hadn't seen her face when she'd told him where she was going. He looked up at the sky. Fill the canteens? Hell, they were about to be deluged with water. He broke into a dead run, mentally calculating the head start he'd given her.

She was easily followed. He was able to catch up with her and close in quietly. By the time she heard him, he was close enough to reach out and grab her by the arm.

"The stream's back this way."

Elizabeth stiffened and refused to turn around. "I've decided to go down there myself, McQuade."

"And do what?"

"Get my son."

He turned her to face him, keeping a firm hold on her upper arms. "I can't let you do that, Elizabeth."

Even in the near-darkness, he could see the fire in her eyes. "What lengths would you go to stop me?"

"I won't hurt you." He moved quickly and smoothly to sling her over his shoulder. "But I won't let you hurt yourself, either. Comfortable?"

"McQuade!"

"If you're worried about my back—"

"This—is—an—outrage!"

"—don't trouble yourself."

"Put me down!"

"I can bench press—"

"I—will not—tolerate this."

"—at least two of you. No problem."

McQuade's understanding of colloquial Spanish was stretched beyond its limits. He gave up counting the number of colorful words Elizabeth used to describe his depravity as he carried her up the hill. When the rain started, it came down in torrents, and he set Elizabeth on her feet, grabbed her hand and sprinted the remaining distance with her at his side. By the time

they reached the ruins, the wind had them staggering
like two drunks.

"Get inside!" McQuade shouted as they made their
way down the steps.

Elizabeth flopped back against the wall just inside
the entryway and fought to catch her breath. Mc-
Quade worked feverishly to clear the pile of rocks and
debris that threatened to trap water in the stairwell. He
sent the offending rubbish down the hill by handfuls
until the water's path was no longer blocked. As he
straightened from his work, the branch of a tree was
caught by the wind and suddenly smacked the back of
his head. Elizabeth gasped at the sight and plunged
back into the wind to help him.

McQuade rubbed his head, hoping the flashing red
and green lights he was seeing weren't signals for a
blackout. He dropped one shoulder against the wall
and fought to clear his mind. He felt a tentative hand
on his back and another touch his hair.

"Is it bad?" she asked.

If he turned around, he knew he would yell at her.
His head throbbed. "It's okay," he answered tightly.
"Can you get the flashlight?"

"It's bad, isn't it?"

"Just get the flashlight, Elizabeth. I'll be okay in a
minute." He listened to the sound of cautious foot-
falls and knew she was battling her fear and winning,
at least for the moment. "It's straight ahead," he
called out to encourage her. "Keep going. You'll run
right into our stuff." He heard a rustling and hoped it
was Elizabeth and not the iguana. His ears welcomed

a click. "Great. A light at the end of the tunnel. Please don't shine it in my face."

She came to him. "Do you feel dizzy?"

"Not really."

"Not *really*?" She slipped her arm around his waist and draped his over her shoulder. "You're not really sure you won't fall flat on your face, are you?"

"To show my good breeding, I'm going to cooperate with you." He didn't lean on her, but he let her steady him, adding, "Just to show you how cooperating is done."

"That was outrageous, Sloan, to carry me that way."

"Yeah, yeah."

"It was boorish."

"Where the hell did you get a word like that? Does it mean anything like stupid?" He sat on the floor and propped his back against the wall. "Because that's what you were being. Plain stupid."

She knelt in front of him. "Obviously I would have turned back when the storm hit."

"Obviously you might not have made it." She shone the light in his eyes, and he turned his face. "Cut that out!"

"I want to see if your pupils are dilated, Sloan. Open your eyes." He complied, and she was relieved to find that his pupils immediately became black pinpricks in a field of stony gray.

He touched the back of his head again. "I've got a real goose egg back here. It's a good sign if it swells up right away like that."

"We need something cold to put on it." She reached into her backpack and came up with a bandanna. "I'll be right back."

Taking the light with her, she went to the door and returned with the bandanna soaked by the cold rain. He held it against the back of his head and closed his eyes, tempted to let the inky swirls behind his eyelids take him where they would. When he looked up, he saw Elizabeth, shivering in the shadows. Her hair was still partly knotted at her nape, partly plastered to the sides of her face. Her skirt and blouse were sopping, as well.

"Change your clothes," he ordered gruffly. "You look like a drowned rat."

"Yours are wet, too." She stood there hugging herself and waiting for the roof to fall in. It amazed her to watch him contain his anger. She hadn't known men who were capable of such control, and she hadn't intended to test this one's limits. There had been a storm coming, Tomás had been just out of reach, and, Lord, she'd only wanted her baby.

It had been a foolish move; she knew that now. She regretted the pain she'd caused McQuade, and although she expected rage any moment, she stepped closer, holding out her hand. "Let me take that out again. It has to be cold."

He came to his feet slowly, unsure of his balance. What did she think he was going to do? She looked like some frightened waif. Hell, he'd brought her to safety, and she looked as though she expected to be thrown to the wolves. He offered the bandanna, but he seized her hand when she tried to take it from him.

"What were you trying to do, Elizabeth? Scare the life out of me?"

Her heart hammered with fear. "All I could think about was Tomás—that he was so close."

"This damned hurricane was closer."

She made a gesture of entreaty with her free hand. "He's just a baby, Sloan. That house could blow away."

"Yeah," he said, nodding. "Yeah, maybe. And what were you gonna do if it did? Don't even think about that, Elizabeth, because if it happens, there's not a damn thing you can do about it. Chances are he's safe." He gripped her wrist more tightly then he intended. "Do you know what *your* chances were out there?"

"Please, let me go," she whispered.

He grabbed her shoulder in his other hand. "What if I hadn't found you? You know what I imagined?" He shook her once. "This delicate little body smashed against a tree somewhere."

"Don't. Please."

"Don't what?" he roared. "Don't sling you over my shoulder like a *boorish* American or whatever the hell else you were calling me out there?"

"Don't shout," she pleaded.

"Why not? Afraid I'll wake the neighbors?"

"I'm afraid—" she closed her eyes "—for my son."

"I told you I'd get him, Elizabeth. Don't you trust me yet? Don't you believe—"

"Yes, I believe," she whispered. "Please, let me go."

He released her, and she took a step back. The look on her face sliced through him, and the pain it caused glistened in his eyes. "God Almighty, woman, do you think I'd hurt you? Don't you know there's only one way I can think of touching you?" He reached for her and pulled her into his arms. "One way," he growled. "And that's *this* way."

She responded to his kiss without reservation because there was no time to think. There was only the need to share, and there was no mistaking his need, nor was there any denying hers. His tongue probed, and hers answered, *Sloan, you taste good, and if you would nourish me, I would devour you.*

He demanded her body's full attention as he held her flush against him and ground his need against hers, as if to say, *Elizabeth, I'd fit you so well, and I'd make your body weep for joy and send your mind soaring.*

She lifted her chin and asked for more of him, pulling at him with her arms, her hands, her mouth. This was a dream changing into demanding need—the need to be kissed passionately and touched gently. And gently he touched her at her back, her bottom, her shoulders. Even with his hands in her hair, there was no pain.

Wet clothes, he thought absently. They have to go. He longed for the feel of her skin against his, the chance to make her warm. He pulled the blouse over her shoulders and down to her waist, hoping she would do the same for him.

She froze.

When he hesitated, she pushed herself away from him, covering herself with one hand and tugging at the elastic neckline of her blouse with the other.

"What's wrong?"

"You can't do this!" Her voice rose with fear.

"Do what? Make love to you?"

She moved away again, and this time McQuade turned his back on her rejection of him. "There's a word for you, lady. How do you say *tease* in Spanish?" Tossing his wet shirt over his backpack, he dug out a pack of cigarettes before he lost his temper out of pure frustration.

He stood at the doorway and mopped the back of his head with rainwater, letting it sluice down his neck and over his back. He needed to soak his whole body in a cold bath. He had let her get to him again. Had he stopped using his head altogether? He was breaking all his own rules—good, solid rules that had kept him out of trouble for years. He draped the bandanna over his neck and lit a cigarette.

Dropping his head back, he leaned against the arch that formed the entry to the underground passage and he dragged smoke deep into his lungs. *Rule number one: A female client is not a woman. Never confuse the two.* He exhaled and remembered *rule number two: Emotions cloud the clearest thinking. Don't indulge in them.* His brain had been clicking along fine, stacking up contingency plans, adding in the variables, and then she'd bolted. God in heaven, he'd drawn a mental blank. He'd raced after her like a lunatic rather than the calculating professional he considered himself to be. Then, when he'd looked at her back there, and she'd flashed him those big brown eyes full of fear... *Rule number three: When you remember the color of her eyes, you're in too deep.*

He laughed aloud, and the wind howled back at him. In too deep? Hell, that was all he really wanted, wasn't it? He wanted to bury himself in her to the hilt. That would satisfy him. She could flash those big brown eyes all she wanted, but once he'd had the satisfaction of breaking the ice barrier, she'd be dealing with a man who was fully in charge of his faculties again.

A tree limb suddenly crashed across the steps above him, and McQuade drew back into the passageway. Then he heard a soft noise at his back, which startled him even more. It sounded like a strangled sob to him, and his first thought was: not Elizabeth, Elizabeth doesn't cry. But the sound tugged at him like a rope. He flicked the cigarette butt into the night's chaos and went to her.

He found her huddled against the wall, clutching the flashlight and crying. When she saw him, she sat up quickly, breathing deeply in an effort to calm herself. She was swiping at her tears with the backs of her fingers when he knelt beside her and gently moved her hand aside. She closed her eyes and let him swab her cheeks with the cool, wet bandana. The hand he held was cold. He massaged it, giving warmth as he absorbed her tremors.

"I'm sorry," he murmured. "Forget what I said. It was...it was boorish as hell."

"No, it wasn't. It was true." She rolled her eyes toward the ceiling and gave a shaky sigh. "In a way it was true," she amended. "I didn't intend to tease you, but it worked out that way, didn't it? And I don't even do that well. Before you can succeed at teasing, you have to succeed at being a woman, and I've...lost touch with that, I think."

"Lost touch with being a woman?" His voice rose in disbelief.

Her eyes were swimming in tears again when she looked at him. "It was so good on the swing, Sloan. I felt free, and our kiss felt like something I could have had once."

"It was something you *did* have, Elizabeth. *We* had it. It was good for me, too. What happened tonight?"

"You were angry." She dropped her head back against the wall and tried to remember the look in his eyes.

"Honey, I was mad as hell. You scared the living daylights out of me."

She saw the echo of that look even now. Anger out of fear, she thought. How strange. "I encouraged you when you kissed me tonight. I know that. I had no right to turn you away after that."

No right? He turned the words over in his mind. They didn't sit well with him, even though he had to admit he had always believed that what she'd said was true.

"Who says?"

The question took them both off guard. Had he really voiced it? Had she really heard it? Elizabeth sniffled, and McQuade handed her the bandanna. "What I mean is that I liked the feeling I got when you . . . when we kissed," she said.

"I could tell."

"But when you started to . . ."

No innocence? Like hell, he thought. "To take your blouse off," he supplied as he shifted and sat down beside her.

"Yes," she said quickly. "I felt differently then."

"Scared?" She nodded. He took the bandanna from her, set it aside and held her hands in his, massaging her palms with his thumbs. "Your hands are always cold, you know that?" Again she nodded. "Why do you think that is?"

"I don't know. I think I'm a cold person."

"You also think you've got all this worldly knowledge, and I don't think you know beans."

She gave him a sidelong glance. "Beans?"

He shrugged. "Just an expression. It means you don't know a damn thing."

She forgave him his arrogance because he couldn't have known what ugliness she carried in her head. If she could shed the years, the pain and the scars right then, there would be no fear, and she would open her arms to him.

"I want to ask you something about your husband."

"Don't—"

"Did he ever kiss you?" She looked at him quizzically, and he didn't like the feeling that he was trespassing where she didn't want him to go. He liked the thought of Guerrero doing anything with Elizabeth even less, but he had a hunch. He swallowed hard. "I mean, you know, like . . . like I did."

"No."

"He never . . . started out by—"

"No. He never did." Her tone said that that was the end of the discussion. She would tell him no more.

But he wasn't willing to accept that.

"How did he start out, then?" She closed her eyes and shook her head. "By pulling off your clothes?"

"Sometimes," she said in a small voice.

"Like I just did?"

"Not . . . not exactly. You were kissing me."

He nodded, letting the image sit in his brain for a minute. He was inclined to ask more questions, but he knew he'd already taken something she hadn't wanted to give.

"I want to do something for you, Elizabeth." He stood and drew her to her feet. "You're cold because your clothes are wet, and I want to help you take them off."

"I can do that myself," she said quietly. The fear came back into her eyes instantly.

He held her gaze with his, willing her to see that he had no hidden intentions as he lifted his hand to the back of her head. With great care he took the remaining pins from her hair. "I want to help you put dry clothes on. And I want to kiss you. And that's all. I promise."

The only warmth she knew at that moment came from his bare chest. She longed to touch him there, to cover his nipples with her fingers, but her hands felt like buckets of cement hanging by her sides.

He combed through her hair with his fingers. "Have I shown you anything to trust in me?" he asked.

"Yes."

"Tell me it's okay, then. I'll stop whenever you say."

"Sloan—"

"I know. You're scared. I want to help you stop being scared."

"I can't...."

"Try," he whispered as he eased her blouse over her head. She hadn't worn a bra because the De Coloran women generally didn't, and she'd dressed as one of them. She hadn't worn one the night on the swing, either, and he'd been tantalized then as he was now. He freed her breasts, but he avoided looking, avoided touching.

"You okay?" he asked. She nodded, wide-eyed, and he smiled. "Breathe, then." He held her shoulders in his hands, and when she'd allowed herself a breath, he covered her mouth with a soft, easy kiss. He slipped his thumbs inside the elastic waistband of her skirt and found her panties in the same motion.

She stood perfectly still while he slid both garments the length of her legs. He figured that only a eunuch could do this with his eyes closed, and, as his eyes passed over each soft curve from breast to knee, he became painfully aware that he was no eunuch. She stepped out of her clothes, but he gripped the fabric in both hands for a moment longer, just to keep himself occupied. Then he brought jeans, panties and a shirt from her backpack. He slid the panties into place first, and then the jeans. His hands weren't quite steady on the snap.

"I've never done this in reverse," he muttered. A brief giggle brought his head up. The wariness was still evident in her eyes, but there was a spark of something warmer, and there was the shadow of a smile. He reached for her shirt and offered her one sleeve at a time as he tried to look anywhere but at her breasts. The challenge was impossible. He pulled the shirt together in front and buttoned it with deliberate motions.

"Are *you* okay?" she asked gently.

He held up his hands, his job done. "Hey, I'm cool as a—" he swallowed the word *cucumber* and fumbled for another choice. He came up with *fruitcake*.

Now she could laugh. "What strange expressions you have, Mr. McQuade."

Her eyes were still red, but there was a smile in them now, and he was smiling back. Under pressure.

"Yeah. Well, it's kind of a mixed metaphor, which means I, uh, need a cigarette. When I come back—"

"You don't have to go out there to smoke."

"Yeah, I do. I'll just take a minute. See if you can find us something to eat. When I come back, we need to talk." He reached up to smooth his hand over her hair. "Friends?"

Sharp tears sprang to her eyes. She nodded and pushed the word past the tightness in her throat. "Friends."

Their underground refuge had become a wind tunnel. McQuade's head still throbbed, and his cigarette wasn't doing that situation any good, but at least it was taking his mind off the rest of his body.

The problem was that he couldn't forget hers. Only a poet could describe the grace of its form and the poignancy of its slightness. He wanted to have her fitted for armor while he sharpened his sword, all for her defense. She brought out such an array of instincts in him, both lofty and base, that he was finding it impossible to conduct himself normally. Normal for him had always meant going with his instincts. He groaned inwardly. Had she screwed those up, too?

She was sitting cross-legged in the middle of her sleeping bag. She'd spread the beds out side by side again, and he settled across from her. Her backpack was close at hand, but she hadn't taken any food out of it.

"Doesn't dried fish catch your fancy?" he asked.

"No. Would you like some?" She reached for the zipper. "I'm sure you must be hungry."

"One of the agreements we made was that you'd follow my instructions on this little jaunt, Elizabeth. Now, I've noticed that you don't eat enough to keep a canary alive, and I've gotta tell you, it shows.'' She looked surprised and a little hurt. He smiled apologetically. ''I couldn't help it. I tried to avert my eyes, but they wouldn't stay averted. You've got to eat something, honey.''

''I did,'' she reminded him. ''I ate Chi Chi's paella. I think she outdid herself for you.''

''Is that why you picked at it like you weren't sure the shrimp were dead?'' She made a face, and he gave her knee a teasing squeeze. ''Thought I might have to kiss the cook, huh?''

''It wasn't that good,'' she said stubbornly.

He reached for the backpack. ''You're going to eat, Elizabeth. It's risky for you not to. Beef jerky.'' She accepted the offer grudgingly. ''It's delicious.''

''I get along on very little food.'' In response to his admonishing glare, she tore off a piece of the dried meat with her teeth. ''Especially when I'm away from home.''

''But this *is* your home,'' he said over a mouthful of jerky. ''Not this pit, but this island.''

Elizabeth nodded, chewing slowly as she considered the idea of ''home.'' ''It was once. It was my mother's home, and my grandmother's. But my father didn't belong here. He used this island as a base for his activities, and he used my mother.'' She swallowed, then studied the food in her hand. Her look of distaste was not for the meat.

''He thought she gave him legitimacy, a plausible reason to be here, and that having a child made him a family man. All for the public eye. But he had no more respect for marriage than he had for the law. He was gone a lot of the time.''

McQuade had a strange, tight feeling inside, the kind he got when he knew he was on the verge of learning a key piece of information, the one that would take him straight to the heart of a case—or, perhaps, a person. He was afraid to move, afraid she would become self-conscious and back off from telling him more.

''It was important to him that his daughter have an American education,'' she continued, ''so I attended prep school and college. He planned to use me as a pawn, to arrange a marriage for me that would give him the berth he wanted in American society.'' She smiled slowly. ''But I spoiled his plan.''

''How?''

''I married Rodolfo Guerrero, the rebel.'' Her short laugh was mirthless, and the sound of it made McQuade feel slightly sick. She continued on a sardonic note. ''I showed my father, didn't I? I married one of my own countrymen, a man who had risen through the ranks of the old regime and then boldly denounced its tyranny.''

''You're talking about *Guerrero*?'' With his thumb McQuade drew a slash beside his left eye and lifted a questioning eyebrow. The scar was Guerrero's most unforgettable feature.

''The same. He was always the same.'' She sighed, shaking her head. ''Only in my *mind* was he ever a man of principle. He left the old regime because the president had agreed to cooperate with the U.S. Drug

Enforcement Agency in an investigation of top De
Coloran officials. Guerrero called it American inter-
vention, but I know now that he was corrupt. He knew
someone would be made a scapegoat to satisfy Washington, and he decided it wouldn't be him.''

"Did Castillo and Hidalgo know all this when they
teamed up with him?''

"General Castillo was Guerrero's uncle. In De
Colores, relatives are forgiven their little shortcom-
ings. Especially the young men, who are expected to
make a few mistakes. The general blamed the system
for Guerrero's corruption and offered him a chance to
redeem himself.''

"How about Hidalgo? Was he a relative?''

"No.''

"Then what's his excuse?''

"He didn't know.'' Elizabeth tipped her head back
and searched the ceiling. Her eyes glistened. "But
more to the point, what was my excuse?''

McQuade touched her knee, which was only a frac-
tion of the gesture he wanted to make. He had to let
her come to him for comfort; otherwise, she would
back away. She needed no excuses with him. He could
blame Castillo, Hidalgo, the whole damned popula-
tion of De Colores, for being taken in by Guerrero, but
not her. And he didn't want her to tell him anything
that would change his mind.

"Elizabeth, what did he do to you?''

She smiled at him as though he were a child who had
touched her heart with an innocent question. "He
didn't force me to marry him. I knew him socially. He

must have seen my need to rebel, and the idea of defying my father along with the other powerful men on the island appealed to him. It also appealed to me. We fled to Central America and were married there. That was five years ago."

"When did he get hooked up with Castillo and Hidalgo?"

"About three years later. He had become quite the revolutionary by then."

"And you?"

She lifted her chin in the dignified way that had once put him off. "I followed my husband until my pregnancy became a burden."

"Oh, God, Elizabeth."

She covered his hand with hers. "I made that choice, Sloan. It was a life I chose when I went with him."

"Elizabeth," he began, and he waited until she looked at him. "Why is such a strong woman so terrified of that man?"

"Are you speaking of me?" she asked. "I'm a very weak woman. Surely you see that." In her shame she glanced away and quietly confessed, "I left my son."

He turned his palm to hers. "He was taken from you, and you were sent away."

"The fact remains—"

"The fact *is* that you are here now in spite of your fear. This is the craziest stunt I've ever seen any woman pull, Elizabeth." His voice grew hoarse. "Every kid's mother should want him that much."

With her free hand, she touched his cheek. She'd watched him shave that morning, and she remembered wondering why he'd gone to such trouble in this situation. With or without stubble, his face invited this gesture. It had become so dear to her.

"I want to make love to you," he whispered. She closed her eyes and gave her head a quick shake. He caught her hand before she withdrew it from his face. "It was your idea to touch me," he said in a low voice. "Don't take that back. I want that."

"You want sex."

"I want to make *love* with you, honey." She shook her head again, and he brought her hand to his mouth and kissed her fingertips. "Why not?" he asked, watching the wildness grow in her eyes. "Tell me why not."

"I couldn't stop you. You know that."

"Yes, you could. All it takes is a word."

"Not when you get..." She scanned the wall behind him, looking for a way out.

"Not when I get what?"

"Not when you get angry," she whispered. "There's nothing that can stop you then."

"And what would I do if I got angry?"

She risked a glance at his face. "You might hurt me. If I didn't do...what you wanted."

McQuade held both her hands, caressing her palms. He struggled to remain outwardly calm. "What do you think I'd want you to do?"

"I don't know," she managed. "I don't remember."

"You don't remember?"

"I couldn't respond," she said quickly. "I hated...I hated..."

"It's okay," he encouraged. "Tell me what you hated."

"It. *Him*. Everything, everything, everything..." She doubled over as if in pain, and he pulled her into his lap. Against her will, she put her arms around him and buried her face against the side of his neck. "I hate myself for being so weak, but I want you to hold me."

"That's not a weakness."

"It is when you want someone else to take care of you, to protect you from—"

"From what?"

"From a choice I made." She tightened her hold on him. "Just hold me," she begged. He did, and she relished the feel of his strength.

"Tell me the rest, Elizabeth."

"I can't."

"You have to tell someone," he said gently. "It's eating you up inside."

"I don't want you to know how weak I am, Sloan." Her voice had become a small thing, and the wind outside seemed to drown it out. But McQuade would have heard had she only mouthed the words. "I don't want you to be disgusted."

"Disgusted?" He was lost in her pain and couldn't think of the right words. "I'm no saint, honey. Why would I be...? Whatever it was, it wasn't your fault."

"If I told you...in your mind, you would see me as—"

"Honey, it doesn't matter," he insisted.

"—totally debased. It matters."

Though she shed no tears, he held her close to his chest and rocked her as if she were crying in torrents. He was afraid his own tears would break loose if he uttered even a single word. Finally she squirmed in his grip. "I have a terrible fear of being smothered," she confided, and his embrace slackened, though he continued to hold her. "If I cried out, he would cover my nose and mouth with his hand or a pillow or something. I blacked out sometimes. He always seemed to know how far he could go without killing me, without breaking a bone or scarring my face. He said...he promised he would never scar my face."

McQuade took a deep breath and exhaled slowly. He couldn't speak.

"You see, Sloan," she whispered. "You don't want to hear any of it. It's disgusting. And weakness—tears and cries for help—those things just bring out more anger in a man."

"Oh, Elizabeth," he groaned. Hot pain warred inside him with cold rage, and he felt almost disoriented. "*You* are not disgusting, and *you* are not weak. And, God help me, I want to tear that bastard limb from limb."

"No. You must never get near him." She remembered the dream, and she hugged him close. "Please, Sloan. There's too much goodness in you, and none in him."

"Don't you believe that good wins out over bad?"

She gave a heavy sigh. "I did believe that, a long time ago, when I was innocent."

"When you can believe it again—" he kissed her forehead and laid his cheek against it "—then I'm sure the nightmares will stop."

"Do you think so? Then I won't be afraid to be alone in the dark."

He reached behind him and flicked off the flashlight. She took a deep breath and held on tight.

"It's dark, and you're not alone," he assured her. "You're not alone at all. You've got good ol' McQuade here."

"Sloan," she said softly.

He chuckled. "Sloan. Right. Who'd have thought it? But if you say I'm good, hell, I'll believe it. And I'm gonna beat the hell out of Rodolfo Guerrero."

Chapter 7

Sloan held Elizabeth through the night, while outside the hurricane did its worst. By midmorning they were enjoying the eye of the storm, a couple of hours of relative calm. The wind was still strong, but they were able to venture outside to wash themselves and get a breath of fresh air. Trees had been uprooted, and the stream had overflowed its banks.

They didn't talk about the destruction the sea must have caused in the low-lying areas. They didn't speculate about conditions in La Primavera and El Gallo, nor did they venture to guess whether there would even be a boat to get them off the island. It occurred to Elizabeth that she might owe Sloan an apology since "his" fisherman had come through for them and "her" pilot had not. It occurred to Sloan that his lack

of judgment in allowing Elizabeth to hire Ronnie
Harper probably deserved some mention. The girl had
probably been scared out somehow. He should have
known that cute little tomboy wasn't up to this kind of
a job. But neither of them spoke of Ronnie. Neither
wanted to risk an argument. This was only the eye of
the storm, and there was more violence to come.

Elizabeth found some undamaged breadfruit and
coconuts near the fallen trees that had produced them.
Fresh delicacies hadn't seemed important before the
storm hit, because they'd been able to go to the village, but they craved them now. They hadn't planned
to spend this much time in the ruins. The hit-and-run
that McQuade had envisioned was not to be.

When the storm unleashed its fury once more,
McQuade looked for ways to keep his hands busy. He
cleaned weapons that were already clean and smoked
the rest of his cigarettes. He put his hands into his
pockets and paced. When he found himself craving
another cigarette, he shoved a stick of gum into his
mouth and paced some more. Finally he let himself
take an interest in the activity Elizabeth had going in
the middle of the floor. Along with the fruit, she'd
gathered some palm fronds, and she was making
something with them.

"Would you like some gum?" he offered as he
squatted beside her on the sleeping bags. She looked
almost content, if not happy, and he thought he might
bribe her to include him.

"I wondered when you'd offer. Thank you."

He stretched out across from her, propping himself on an elbow. "God, I hate this dead time. So what are you up to?"

"I'm weaving a hat. I thought you might like a souvenir of your vacation on De Colores."

"Hell of a vacation. Rained the whole time we were there." He watched her work the palms, weaving them in and out as a circular form took shape. "How do you do that?"

She moved over a little, setting the whole process up under his nose. She demonstrated the basic pattern, and then indicated that he should give it a try. "Do you think your guns are clean enough yet?" she asked.

"The whole arsenal's in great shape," he told her. "I would be, too, if I weren't going stir-crazy. Show me that part again. Like this?"

Her long fingers manipulated the palm leaves, pausing for him to follow, and then went through the motions slowly once more.

"I've got it now," he told her. She let him take over so she could start another one. "Think we could go into the hat business?" he said, snapping his gum with the confident grin of a kid showing off for his coach.

Elizabeth smiled down at her project. "It depends on how long we're stuck in this cave."

"Hey, we could do cave paintings," he suggested, his voice on the rise. "That's how the cavemen spent the winter. What could we use for paint?"

"What did the cave dwellers use?"

"Hell, I don't know—berry juice, clay, blood, maybe." His eyes lit up. "Iguana blood! We'll set a trap."

"This stir-craziness seems to bring out your primitive instincts."

"No kidding." He glanced up, wondering whether she knew how close to the truth she was, but she kept working. "Listen to that wind out there, Elizabeth. Imagine how that must've sounded to a caveman."

"About the same way it sounds to me."

He watched her for a moment and then tried to remember whether he was looping over or under. "So they found something to distract themselves, like making spears, arrows, babies—stuff like that."

"Be careful, Sloan." She raised a prim eyebrow. "You promised to remain as cool as a fruitcake. No Freudian slips, please." She gestured vaguely in his direction. "Keep that part up."

His youthful innocence had vanished, and he gave her a slow, glittering grin. "That's just the trouble, honey. Why do you think I've been wearing a hole in the carpet?"

She reached for the end of the frond he held in his hand. "This," she directed with exaggerated patience. "Up. This loops under." He was still grinning at her. "You're absolutely outrageous, Sloan McQuade."

"You've heard of the spears and arrows of outrageous fortune?"

"*Slings* and arrows," she corrected.

"No way, lady. This is my Freudian slip, caveman style, which calls for *spears*." She shook her head, but he thumped his bare chest with his fist in triumph. He had her laughing. "Let's sacrifice an iguana and paint the walls with naked women wearing palm hats. Otherwise I'm about to become as nutty as a cucumber."

"Cucumbers aren't nutty, not even American cucumbers." McQuade rolled over on his back and gave his whole body over to laughter. "I ought to know," Elizabeth insisted. "I had them by the dozens in Miami."

"Did you, now?" He rolled his head and grinned up at her. "You're playing with me, aren't you? I love it."

She offered a coy smile. "I'm teaching you to weave hats, but you're a very inattentive pupil."

"You're right." Affecting seriousness, he sat up and attended to what he was doing. "We've got to get this done before winter sets in. Probably won't need too many spears and arrows."

"Not with the automatic revolver and whatnot."

"*Semi*automatic *pistol*, and who's an inattentive pupil?" A light dawned in his eyes. "Hey, that's what we should do!" Tossing her hat aside, he reached for his backpack. "How about a munitions lesson? I want you to be able to load and fire the .38."

Her hands stilled as she watched him take a handful of bullets from a box, arrange them in a row in front of him and then bring out the revolver. "I don't think I want to," she said quietly.

He glanced up at her and dismissed her objection. "Look, if I have some confidence in your ability to protect yourself, I can concentrate on protecting Tomás. Make sense?'' With a sigh, she nodded. He patted the place beside him on their pallet. "Come on over here, then.'' He adjusted the beam from the flashlight while she settled next to him.

With a click of the release, the cylinder swung into his hand. ''Slide the cartridges into the chambers, slick and easy. You get six shots, see? This is the safety. It's on now, so you can't shoot anybody. Off, it's ready to fire.'' He glanced up to see whether she was following him. Satisfied that she was he continued, manipulating each feature as he explained its purpose. ''You use the ejection rod to unload the cartridges, like this. You always check to see if it's loaded, even if you think you're sure. You don't take my word for it, or rely on your memory. You check it out. Understand? I don't want you to hurt yourself with this thing.'' She nodded. ''Okay, load it yourself, then, just like I showed you.''

He handled the weapon as easily as he would a bottle of bourbon, but in her hands it became a delicate object, a piece of fragile equipment. She went through the motions carefully, and he decided she might be able to return fire half an hour after somebody had shot at her. She worked at it for a while, and then they took a break, trading their gum for the taste of coconut milk. Returning to the lesson, he made her repeat the loading process until she could do it in a matter of seconds. When she no longer handled the revolver as though she were trying to balance a handful of fresh eggs, it was time for step two.

"Now for some target practice," McQuade announced.

Elizabeth scowled at him. "I'm not shooting this thing in here."

"Unload it, and show a little respect. It's a revolver, not a thing, and it could save your life. Or mine, or Tomás's, if you're covering us." The stony look he gave her made her shiver. They were no longer playing. "We're all in this together, and we can't afford the luxury of being squeamish."

"I am not squeamish. I'm just…" She squared her shoulders as she snapped the empty cylinder into place and checked the safety. Then she lifted both her chin and her gun hand purposefully. "I need a target," she said, looking toward the doorway.

He aimed the smaller of the two flashlights at the wall, and then he moved behind her. "Are you right-eyed or left-eyed?" he asked. She turned a frown his way. "I suppose you wouldn't know that, huh? Let's close the left and sight down the barrel with the right. Both arms straight, the left supports the right. This is the sight, right here." He touched the metal tab on the nose of the barrel and steadied her arm. "You can pull the hammer back with your thumb for more accuracy, or just use the trigger. Try it."

She cocked the hammer and pulled the trigger, producing an empty click. He wasn't satisfied. "Just squeeze with your finger, honey, not your whole hand. When you fire, it makes a lot of noise, because it has a short barrel, but it won't recoil too much, because it's a small-caliber weapon. You have to be fairly close to the target. Try again.''

He enjoyed laying his cheek next to hers, sighting down the barrel with her, taking physical control and leading her step by step. He got her to stand up and go through the process again. ''Just squeeze with your finger,'' he repeated. ''You're not milking a cow. Deep breath and hold it. Do it like you mean it. This isn't a toy.''

He would have liked to be a toy in her hands himself about then. She was beginning to relax with the weapon and move smoothly, and that excited him. If she would only squeeze him instead, he could promise he wouldn't recoil. He bit off the suggestion he wanted to make by nuzzling delicately at her jaw, just beneath her ear. ''You're doing great,'' he muttered.

''It's not so bad,'' she decided, examining the .38 once more. His breath felt deliciously warm against her neck. As long as he stood behind her that way, she would have practiced until her arms fell off.

''Of course, it *is* unloaded,'' he admitted.

''And the target is only a beam of light. If it were a man . . .''

''If the man had a gun, Elizabeth, and if it were pointed at you—'' he took her shoulders in his hands and turned her to face him ''—or Tomás, or even me . . .''

''I would have to shoot, wouldn't I? I would have no choice.'' No choice, she thought, wondering if such a situation truly existed. ''Does it make it any easier

later, when you think back on it, to know you did it
because you had to?''

He wanted to freeze the moment. His answer would
have come easily if she'd asked if he'd ever killed a
man. That he had, was a matter of record. But she'd
asked him how he felt about it, and the answer to that
wasn't on record anywhere—yet.

''It's never easy to think back on it,'' he confessed
quietly.

''How do you ever know? When you look back,
how do you know that you *had* to do something?'' He
hung his head, and she knew he didn't have the answer, either. ''If our lives were in danger,'' she ventured. ''Tomás's, yours, or mine...''

''You could use it, then?''

''I think so.'' She looked up at him, and, just for a
moment, he saw past her eyes and into her soul.
''When something unspeakable must be done, we
block it out, and we go through the motions to sur-
vive.'' She touched his cheek. ''Don't we, Sloan?''

''Yeah. I guess we do.''

He took the revolver from her hand and studied it
while unwelcome images, some vivid, some shadowy,
flickered through his mind. He'd lived thirty-six years,
and he'd done his share of living. There was a lot he
didn't like thinking about, a lot he wouldn't tell her,
because he wouldn't want her thinking about it, either.
Tucking the .38 into the back of his waistband, he
looked down at her again, his eyes mirroring that
touchstone of the human condition, the skeleton that
rattled in every mind's closet. He understood now that

it was enough to be able to admit to another person simply that it was there. He didn't need the details of her memories, and she didn't his.

"I don't spend too much time looking back anymore," he told her. "I know it sounds like that's easy to say. It's not." He lifted her chin in his cupped hand. "You've got your nightmares. I've got mine. But I'd gladly kill that bastard, Guerrero, and take on another one if it would set your mind free."

"That's not the answer," she whispered. "Just get me my son."

"I will. And then what? That's not the only answer, is it?"

"I don't know what you mean."

"Yes, you do. There's more to this nightmare of yours, and we need another answer." He drew her into his arms and lowered his head, promising, "I'm damn well gonna find it."

He took her to their bed and made her dizzy with his kisses, but he made no demands as he held his needs in check. His lips moved over hers slowly, savoring her like a discriminating gourmet. Her lips parted for him, and the kiss sweetened. Oh, she was good. But he told himself it was enough just to touch her, to have her reach around him of her own volition and lay her cool hands on his back. He knew the answer he was looking for lay in giving, not making demands.

She stilled his hand when he unbuttoned the top button on her shirt, but he bade her, "Trust me. I just want to kiss you, honey. I just want to touch you and give you pleasure."

"There is no—"

"Yes, there is. Let me show you." He waited until she released his hand, and then he freed her breasts, caressed them, kissed them, made them harden with need. It was impossible not to touch her gently. Her femininity made his masculine protectiveness surge to the fore. He would let no harm come to her, least of all at his own hands, and she would learn that no part of his attentions needed to be dreaded. Then she would respond to him fully, and, please, God, she would respond without fear.

She moaned, and his name on her lips became a plea. For what? For more? For mercy? His body reminded him of his own needs, and he struggled to contain them. He loved a challenge; scaling the wall of Elizabeth's fear was the ultimate test. Each time he touched her in a new place, she stiffened against him.

"Easy, baby," he whispered when she stopped him from unzipping her jeans. "It doesn't have to hurt. Let me show you."

She shut her eyes tight against the war going on inside her. His gentle touch was an alien thing, but it claimed to be her body's friend. Her senses were not to be believed, she decided. She had to get away from him, yet she wanted to become part of him. Experience had taught her to be still, to endure. But an untried part of her wanted to enjoy.

"Don't try to prove anything," she ground out. "Just get it over with."

Something inside him was angry. Something else was hurt, and something was sad. He moved past all those things, because caring consumed all else and gave him power over his impulses. Pressing himself against her hip, he let her feel his need while managing to deal with it in his own head. Her need was greater.

"Get it over with? Put your arms around my neck, and I will," he promised. When she complied, he whispered, "Kiss me, and I will." She opened her lips to his kiss as he slid his hand under her jeans and over her belly. He found soft fabric, softer skin, and the contrasting coarseness that protected the place he most wanted to touch. Skilled fingers made her moist, made her moan against his mouth, made her arch into his hand and call his name. The plea was unmistakable this time.

"Come to me, sweetheart." He watched her. Her eyes were closed, but the tension drained from her face as she gave herself over to him. She was lovely.

"It feels...oh, Sloan..."

"Good," he whispered, and he kissed the corner of her mouth. "It's good."

Her arms tightened around his neck, and she affirmed, "It's good."

"You want me to...get it over with?"

"No," she breathed. Then, "Yes! It's too..."

"Too good? Go with it, honey. I'm with you...all the way."

"Too good," she said, and her overwhelming shudder took her with him. The smell of her, the feel of what was happening under his hand, the flushed beauty of her face, gave his body leave to share. Ordinarily he might have cursed. Tonight he kissed the woman who had given him more than pleasure. She had trusted him.

"That's never happened before," she said shyly.

He smoothed her hair back from her face. "It will again. I promise. When you're ready."

"But what about you? What did you get?"

"I don't have to 'get.' I want you to give."

"What if I can't?"

Smiling, he slipped an arm beneath her shoulders and lay down, holding her in his arms. "Too late. You already have."

The rain ceased, and the wind blew itself out by midmorning. The rushing stream chased the effects of inertia from McQuade's body and made his skin tingle. For Elizabeth, a heightened awareness of her skin's sensitivity had blossomed hours before. She was afraid to speak of it lest she lose it in the light of day. The cold water brought delicious renewal.

Now she faced a day of reckoning. The trek down the mountainside bred pure dread. It was as if huge jaws had torn the lush tropical island to shreds and spat it out in a shambles. Many buildings had been damaged, some totally razed to the ground. McQuade watched as Elizabeth took everything in, and he shared her fears in silence. They reached the road to El Gallo, and at a spot that had once been a picturesque overlook, they stopped to survey the town.

The cantina looked unscathed, as did the sturdier structures—the community center, the one small store in town and a few of the houses. But the rest—the storage Quonset, the tin-roofed huts—were all in varied states of destruction. So much of the vegetation was in shreds that it looked as though a herd of huge beasts had grazed there.

At the sound of an approaching vehicle, they dove into the brush for cover. A truckload of armed soldiers rumbled by them. When it had passed, Elizabeth moved to stand, but McQuade caught her arm. They waited while two jeeps and another truck sped by. After several quiet minutes had lapsed, McQuade turned his attention to El Gallo again. He realized that it was now crawling with soldiers.

"Elizabeth," he began, "I'm taking you back to the ruins. I want you to wait there for me."

"I'm going with you."

Her chin was high, and her jaw was set. He knew she wasn't going to make this easy. "If we're picked up, you can forget about rescuing your son. If I'm alone and I'm picked up, I've got Red Cross identification and people who'll vouch for me." He took her by the shoulders and made her look at him. "You agreed to do as I said, and I'm saying you can't go down there. I'll check in with Emilio and see if he's still got a boat. Then I'll find Tomás." She lowered her eyes, doubting him, and he tightened his grip on her. "I swear I will. For God's sake, have some faith in me."

"I do," she said softly. "If it can be done, you'll do it."

"It can be done. This won't be easy on you, I know, but you'll have to wait—'' he cast a glance at the mountain ''—up there.''

"Sloan—''

"You're going to handle this, honey, and I'm going to know you're safe. I'll get Emilio to pick us up on the other side of the mountain, where he let us off.''

"What if his boat was damaged by the storm?''

"I'll find another one.'' He knew he was asking her to believe the myth that he could work miracles. Right now, he needed to believe it himself. "I'm taking you back. You with me?''

On impulse, she slid her arms around his waist and held him close. His arms came around her, too, just for a moment, and then he said, "Let's go.''

Leaving her at the ruins wasn't any easier on Mc-Quade than it was on Elizabeth. She kissed him hard before he set out again, and the desperation in that gesture shook him. She was counting on him. He'd always taken his jobs seriously, but he took this one to heart. The loss of his objectivity put a new wrinkle in the execution of his plan. Ordinarily he reserved the option of pulling out when the risk factor became too overwhelming. This time he knew damn well he was going in without allowing himself that option.

He was challenged by two soldiers when he entered the village, but his Red Cross identification got him past them. Outside the cantina he ran into Emilio.

"I am getting ready to leave, McQuade. According to the reports, the hurricane bypassed Arco Iris and is headed for Florida.''

McQuade clamped a hand on the shorter man's husky shoulder. "That must mean *La Paloma* is still seaworthy."

"My brother and I beached her before the storm hit," Emilio told him. "He was going to help me scrape her hull in return for a load of fish. She was in a sheltered place."

McQuade cast his eyes heavenward and grinned. "Somebody up there likes me."

"But we're putting out to sea before the army decides to confiscate her. So many of the boats here were destroyed."

"Listen, Emilio, I'm going to make you a rich man." Emilio made a move to back away, but McQuade tightened his grip. "I'm going over to La Primavera to find the child we came here for. Elizabeth is waiting for me on the mountain. You meet us in the same spot where you dropped us off. Pick us up about midnight. You'll have to paddle ashore for us. Do you have another raft?"

"I can get one," he said hesitantly. "A child?"

McQuade nodded. "It means his life, Emilio." The man who anticipated becoming a father was not about to refuse. "I'll help you get your boat out of here, *amigo.*"

Within another hour McQuade was on his way to La Primavera. He'd seen Emilio's fishing boat safely out to sea and had secured a pack of cigarettes from the cantina as an afterthought. He avoided roads, but every moment was precious now. He couldn't expect Emilio to risk waiting for them, and there was so much to do by midnight. He found a town that was reeling from the shock of a hard blow to the gut. People were picking through the rubble of what, just days before, had been an easygoing life-style. Soon they would pull together and begin licking their communal wounds, but now they were dazed.

The army was out in force. McQuade had to produce his identification twice as he made his way through the narrow streets toward the address he'd been given for Maria Adelfa, Tomás's nurse. He had the child carrier in his pocket and his pistol tucked at his back in the waistband of his pants.

A police car cruised by, announcing over its loudspeaker a five o'clock curfew and the locations of shelters for those whose homes had been destroyed. The officer slowed for a second look at the tall Anglo whose short-sleeved bush jacket billowed behind him. The policeman was looking for potential looters, and the jacket could easily be concealing a weapon. He paused to get a look at the man's face. Then he smiled.

"McQuade! *¿Qué pasa?* This is no time for a vacation, *amigo*. The bars are all closed."

"Hey, Felipe! I forgot to check the weather report before I came down here." McQuade remembered the young man as one who had generally been on cussing terms with the law, but he'd also usually been good for cheap bits of information. The car crawled along beside him as McQuade continued to walk. Felipe was apparently anxious for a friendly chat, and McQuade didn't want to arouse any suspicions. "How the hell did you get into a cop's uniform?"

The man shrugged. "New government, new opportunities. What brings you down this time of year, McQuade? You know it's hurricane season."

"Came in with a load of Red Cross supplies." At least it had started out that way, he thought. "My pilot took a powder. Cute little redhead—keeps her hair tucked up under a baseball cap. Ronnie Harper. What do you know about her?"

"Not a thing, man. Maybe she took off with a load of something a little hotter than Red Cross supplies."

"Nah, I doubt it." He'd considered that possibility, too, but he'd rejected it simply because he refused to be that wrong. They were nearing the Red Cross office, where he hoped he'd find the one woman in the world he knew damn well he could count on. "This looks like my stop, Felipe. I'll try to stay out of trouble."

"You do that." He lowered his voice and leaned out the window. "If you're doing any snooping around, McQuade, my advice is—don't."

McQuade stood to watch the patrol car pull out into the street and continue on its way before he ducked into the Red Cross office. It was busy, but he managed to corner the small, gray-haired lady who was in charge and spirit her into the back room before she could sputter her initial question too loudly.

"McQuade! What are you doing here?"

He closed the door to the little room he'd used more than once as his office in De Colores. He and Dorothy had an understanding: she gave him a legitimate reason to be there, one that was seldom questioned, and he helped her with her list of concerns, which generally involved detainees or missing persons.

"As far as the government is concerned, I'm working with you guys," he said. "I flew in on a puddle jumper before the storm hit," he lied.

"And why are you really here?"

He could see the worry in her face, and he knew some of it was for him. Dorothy liked to think of herself as an adoptive mother, and of McQuade as one of her many children. "What's it been like here since Castillo died?" he asked.

"Everything's happened so fast. First Castillo, then Hidalgo. I see more uniforms every day. If you're up to something Guerrero might take exception to..." She shook her head. "But then, he takes exception to everything. There are new directives every day, and he declared martial law the day Colonel Hidalgo was assassinated. Don't do anything foolish, McQuade."

"I'm here to find a kid for his mother."

Dorothy's eyes widened. "Not... not Guerrero's child? The mother was—"

"Exiled. Right. I need a favor."

"McQuade—"

He held up his hand. "Just leave the back door unlocked. If the kid objects to keeping company with me, I may need a sedative for him. Will you handle it for me?" Dorothy hesitated. "The kid needs his mother, Dorothy. And Elizabeth needs him."

The very act of uttering her name had softened McQuade's normally stony face.

"I take it this Elizabeth has become important to you."

"She's a client," McQuade claimed.

The woman gave him a maternal smile. "Uh-uh, McQuade. This is Dorothy, who knows you well."

He rolled his eyes and tried to shrug her concern off, but she wasn't buying. "Okay, yeah, this job's different. Without that kid, she'll never be able to—" McQuade shook his head, hoping to clear it of emotion. "She left her son, but she's gone to a lot of trouble to come after him. There isn't much time, Dorothy, and we need your help."

She took a small ring of keys from her pocket and handed him one. "I'll watch out for you," she promised. "But a man carrying a crying child shouldn't arouse too much suspicion out there. People have been bringing them in all day."

Bouncing the key in his hand, he tossed her a wink. "Thanks, beautiful."

Several blocks from the Red Cross office, McQuade found Maria Adelfa's house, or what was left of it. The roof had caved in, and at the sight of the wreckage, McQuade's chest nearly did the same. He stepped over a piece of picket fence, dreading what he might find behind the door.

"Señor McQuade!"

The voice came from around the corner of the house. Dusk was falling on the tattered island, and McQuade turned to peer into the shadows of what had been a small garden. He saw a woman looking at him.

He immediately recognized her as Juanita, Maria's housekeeper and Chi Chi's friend.

"Antonio sent me. I was here when we evacuated, but I went home to El Gallo right after the storm."

"Evacuated? Where?"

"Maria's daughter lives in a house made of poured concrete," she told him. "She took the boy there."

McQuade glanced at the wreckage and shuddered. "Guerrero doesn't care much what happens to his kid, does he? Why didn't he take them to the palace?"

Juanita shrugged. "Maria always goes to her daughter's at the first sign of bad weather. Guerrero might not even know where they are."

Things were looking up, McQuade decided. If he got a move on, he might make it to the boat on time. "Show me the way, Juanita."

Halfway there, Juanita spotted an old woman hurrying down the street with a child bundled in her arms. It was nearly dark, but the woman's familiar waddle caught the girl's attention. "That's her!" She ran ahead of McQuade calling, "Maria!"

McQuade followed, pulling Juanita back to his side as they approached the woman. "Let me handle it," he said quietly as he reached inside his jacket for his identification. "Señora Adelfa, I'm with the Red Cross."

While the old woman peered uncomprehendingly at the papers, the child in her arms studied McQuade, who smiled automatically. Tomás, he thought. Elizabeth's Tomás. Eyes like big black saucers gave a look that said, "So, who are you, mister?"

"She can't read, *señor*," Juanita said.

McQuade's attention snapped back to the old lady. He pointed to the paper. "Here, can you see the cross? It's past curfew, *señora*. You should return to your daughter's house. I'm afraid yours is . . . heavily damaged."

"My house?" Maria looked úp at him, desolation in her voice as she repeated, "My house?"

"I'm sorry, *señora*. I came to get the boy. We're inoculating the children first. Typhoid, you know."

Maria looked at the child as though she weren't certain anymore who he was. "Typhoid?"

"The disease, *señora*. Typhoid. The water system—" The woman turned her blank stare back on McQuade. "*Señora*, I must take the boy to the clinic. His father, the, uh, general—" He glanced at Juanita and knew he had it right. Guerrero had promoted himself. "The general asked me to see to this personally. This is Tomás Guerrero, right?" The old woman nodded. When McQuade reached for the child, Tomás turned away, squealing, but Maria relinquished him automatically, as if she were too stunned by McQuade's news to realize what she was doing.

"My house has been . . . destroyed?" Maria moved past them in a daze, while Tomás squirmed in McQuade's arms and whimpered.

"Go back to your daughter's house, *señora*."

Maria ignored McQuade's instructions. "I'll take her back," Juanita promised. "You take the boy. *Tenga cuidado.*"

"You take care, too," he said. "You forget my name, I'll forget yours."

Tomás's whimpers were turning into pathetic sobs. McQuade kept moving, talking quietly all the while, and by the time he let himself in the back door of the Red Cross building, the sobs were hiccuping little whimpers again.

"Here we go, tiger," McQuade crooned. "We'll get you something to help you sleep, and then I'll take you to your mom. How's that?" He pulled the shade down and turned a desk lamp on. "What else do you need, hmm? What do you wear for shorts?" A pat on the baby's bottom reassured him. "You're a big boy, huh?"

Dorothy appeared at the door. Tomás reassessed his situation, looking from the strange woman to the man who held him, and decided to bury his face in McQuade's jacket. McQuade's chest tightened, and he chuckled as he covered the child's back with a comforting hand.

"It's okay, son. She's a kindhearted old battle-ax."

"He won't think so when I give him this."

McQuade grimaced at the sight of the syringe. "Can't you give him a pill or something?"

"How much time have you got?" Because she knew the answer, she dug under the boy's blanket and found his thigh. "It'll just take a second. Hold him still."

Tomás's howl was thin and brief.

"Sorry, tiger. It's all over now. She won't hurt you again." McQuade ruffled the thick thatch of soft black hair and glanced at Dorothy. "I need some wide adhesive tape."

"And a diaper," she decided.

"Hey, come on, he's got his pride." McQuade looked down at the teary brown eyes. "You wouldn't leak on me, would you?"

"You've got a lot to learn about babies, McQuade." But she had the feeling he was willing.

With the sleeping Tomás strapped to his back in the canvas baby carrier, McQuade slipped through the darkened streets of La Primavera and into the bush. He'd put tape over the baby's mouth to muffle any cries, and he moved quietly toward the mountain. As he traveled, he thought of Elizabeth. His night goggles helped him find his way, but it was dark on the mountain, and, even with a flashlight, Elizabeth was bound to be battling her terrors. She had the revolver, and she knew how to use it, but this must have been an awful day for her. She was one gutsy lady, he thought. One beautiful, gutsy lady.

The closer he got, the faster he traveled. Anticipating her joy, he moved on cat feet, eating up ground in stealthy silence. The night breeze was a gentle echo of the howling wind that had passed. The climb became steeper, and he knew he was on the last leg of the journey. Elizabeth would be waiting at the top of the hill, and McQuade was about to make her a very happy woman. That knowledge made his heart feel light enough to float him to the crest of the mountain.

He flew down the stone steps calling her name, but when he reached the entry, he realized there was no light inside. An icy feeling crept over him. He drew out his pistol and his flashlight.

"Elizabeth?"

Except for their belongings, the underground room was empty.

Chapter 8

McQuade carefully searched the area surrounding the ruins. He brought his panic under control and summoned his skills, combing the territory in widening circles as he risked calling Elizabeth's name. She wasn't there, and time was short. She was either in El Gallo or La Primavera. He worked hard to drive the image of Elizabeth in Guerrero's hands from his mind. He had to be able to think straight—with his brain, instead of with his seething gut. More than once she'd reminded him that she was hiring him to get Tomás off the island no matter what else happened. If he was to accomplish that safely, it had to be done now. Once the boy was discovered missing, he would become one hot property.

His slight hope of finding her waiting for him on the beach was dashed by the same waves that washed the empty shoreline. The child he carried on his back still slept as McQuade climbed down from the rocks and searched the dark horizon. The boat was there. He signaled with his flashlight, and the signal was returned. Fifteen minutes later Emilio paddled a rubber raft to within a few yards of the shore, and McQuade waded out to meet him, carrying his pistol high over his head, the child on his back.

"I have a small life jacket for the baby," Emilio announced. "Where's the woman?"

McQuade searched his brain for the least alarming answer as he backed up to the raft. "Take him, Emilio. We got our signals crossed. I have to go back and find her. Can you wait?"

Emilio worked at the straps on the baby carrier. "I've seen one patrol boat already. We cut the engines and drifted, and he turned back. We have to get out while we can."

McQuade stood waist-deep in the water and felt as though he were drowning. "Can you wait just a couple of hours?"

Taking the baby in his arms, Emilio gave his answer gently, knowing what it meant. "For my family's sake, I must refuse, *señor*."

McQuade hauled himself over the raft's inflated rim and tucked the pistol away. "I'll help you get back to the boat. I need to talk to your wife about taking care of Tomás." He supported the sleeping child between his legs while he put the life jacket on him. Emilio watched, impressed by the care the big man took in peeling the tape away from Tomás's mouth.

Cradling the child in the V of his thighs, McQuade took up a paddle. "If you need the raft, you'll have to paddle me back in. I'm in no mood for a midnight swim."

"You're staying?"

"I'm sure as hell not leaving her here."

Elizabeth had put up a valiant struggle against the encroaching underground walls, but they had finally overwhelmed her. Outside, she'd huddled next to a crumbling wall and watched the night draw down and envelop her. Sloan had been gone too long, she decided. Something had gone wrong. She had no idea how long it should have taken, but the waiting had become unbearable. She needed to move, to act against her fears. She knew where Emilio's brother lived, where the boat had been docked and where Maria Adelpha's house was. She dressed in her skirt and blouse, covered her hair with a scarf and returned to El Gallo.

No one would speak of Emilio, and Elizabeth couldn't locate Antonio. Everywhere people were busy sorting through the rubble and tacking their lives back together with hammer and nails. In La Primavera the story was different. Policemen cruised the streets, and soldiers patrolled, but Elizabeth witnessed several acts of looting as she hurried to her destination. There were other witnesses, as well, but, like Elizabeth, they had more pressing matters to attend to. The cries of those whose houses were unprotected were less urgent than of those who were homeless.

Elizabeth heard such a cry as she approached Maria Adelpha's battered house. The old woman's monotonous moaning drifted softly over the ruins. Elizabeth found Maria bent over a hutch that had been overturned by the winds, its contents smashed over what had once been her porch. Elizabeth's heart forgot its own troubles for a moment and yearned toward her great-aunt.

"*Tía*, you mustn't stay here." She reached for Maria's shoulders, but the old woman ignored her, refusing to straighten. "There are thieves running all over the city, *Tía*. It's not safe for you to be here. These things are all broken."

"All broken," Maria echoed. "All gone."

"*Por favor, Tía*. Where is Tomás?"

The old woman stood then and looked at Elizabeth for the first time. Perhaps because there was so little light, she decided it wasn't worth the effort of trying to figure out who the younger woman was. She sighed heavily and gave all her efforts over to the name. "Tomás?"

"The little boy you're caring for. Where is he?"

Maria shook her head slowly. It was too hard to think about these things now. "Some men took him," she said finally.

"Men in uniforms?"

Maria shrugged and bent down to the ground. As she began sifting through unrecognizable pieces once again she repeated, "Some men."

Elizabeth regretted leaving the old woman in the rubble of her home, but her time was growing short. She had no doubt that Guerrero had sent "some men" to get Tomás and take him to the palace. McQuade might have gone there, too. The risk was awful, but she would have to go herself. She could only hope that pandemonium ruled there, as it did in the streets.

Elizabeth kept to the alleys at first. A door flew open as she hurried along, and she jumped behind a rack of garbage cans. She heard a scuffle, and she flattened her back against the cool stucco wall behind her. There were shouts, the report of gunfire and retreating footsteps. When it was quiet again, she ventured forth and found a man's body lying near the open door. Elizabeth turned and ran.

On the street once again, Elizabeth whirled toward the voice on the loudspeaker. She ducked into a doorway as a police car crawled by. The man might be alive, she thought. Someone should be told.

"*¡Escuche!* Listen! The five o'clock curfew is in effect. All citizens must go home or find shelter. Violators will be arrested."

Then she couldn't tell the police. She couldn't allow herself to be arrested. Moving on, Elizabeth dashed from doorway to doorway, taking a few seconds in each one's dark shelter to check behind her and scan ahead. Power for the street lights had obviously been lost, but the night sky was bright with stars, and occasional headlights flooded the street as a patrol car or an army jeep cruised by.

"*¡Ay! ¡Ay!*"

Elizabeth jumped back in shock from the soft thing she'd stepped on in the narrow doorway of a corner shop.

"¡Discúlpeme, por favor!" she whispered, begging a pardon from whoever lurked in the shadows.

"Get out of here! This place is mine."

"A man has been shot in the alley back there," Elizabeth said quickly. "I don't know whether he's alive, but—"

"Take your trouble somewhere else, woman. Go on!"

She rounded the corner in terror. A beam of light flashed in her eyes, and she covered her face with her hands.

"Identify yourself."

"M-Maria An-Antonio," Elizabeth managed.

"Prove it."

"I can't. My house is a shambles. I've lost—"

"You are in violation of the curfew."

Elizabeth squinted into the light, trying to see the face that went with the harsh voice, but she saw only the outline of a hat. "I . . . can't find my—"

"We have orders to arrest all violators, *señora.*"

"But I must—" Elizabeth stiffened when the man seized her arm. *"Por favor,"* she whispered desperately.

"As soon as your identity is confirmed, you will be assigned to a shelter," he assured her, his voice softening on a note of sympathy.

"Where are you taking me?"

"To the presidential palace."

Assisted by two young soldiers, Elizabeth climbed into the back of a canvas-topped lorry and took a place among the looters and other curfew violators. She was grateful for the soldier who helped pull her into the truck and then ordered a man to get off the bench so she could sit down. Her knees felt as though they might give way beneath her. Raw terror churned in her stomach and threatened to make her physically ill. No one spoke as the truck lurched into motion. The passengers pitched from side to side each time the obviously inexperienced driver shifted gears, but in the intervals they tried to keep their shoulders from touching. It was dark, and they were all strangers.

The truck was unloaded in the palace courtyard. Elizabeth surveyed her surroundings as she was lifted from the truck by the same soldier who had found her a seat. The courtyard lights were off, but several areas were brightened by battery-operated spotlights. Elizabeth avoided those, immediately seeking a dark corner where several women huddled with their children. She could see light in some of the palace windows, which told her that the emergency generator was working. Were they keeping Tomás in the family wing? she wondered. If so, the best route for her would be through the darkened courtyards and gardens, since the troops seemed to be occupied out here in front.

A booming loudspeaker brought all the bowed heads up. "You will all be questioned in due time. Be prepared to prove your identity."

A stout woman near Elizabeth whined, "I have no identification. My purse was stolen."

"It serves you right!" another returned. "You were too busy stealing from my shop."

"One bracelet, and it was lying out in the street. Here, take the worthless thing."

"No," the shop owner said stubbornly. "It is evidence."

The large woman turned to Elizabeth, holding the gold bracelet out to her. "I *found* it," she insisted. "I didn't steal it."

Elizabeth looked at the shop owner. "If all she took was this, the kind thing would be to take it back and say nothing. We've all suffered enough."

The shop owner eyed the bracelet in the other woman's beefy hand, peered into her round face and then accepted the return of her property. "You'd better stay out of my shop," she muttered as she turned away.

"Gracias," the woman whispered to Elizabeth. "I am Serita Martinez, but I can't prove it. Who are you?"

"I am Maria Antonio, but I can't prove that, either."

Serita looked back over her shoulder and then turned a saucer-eyed look at Elizabeth. "Do you think she'll tell?"

"I don't think so. These are dangerous times, Serita. You must be careful."

Serita nodded sadly. "It was so pretty. If I hadn't picked it up, it might have been kicked into the gutter."

"She's lucky you found it for her."

Offering a tentative smile, Serita asked, "What do you think they'll do to us here?"

"I don't know." But Elizabeth had some idea. She'd been held with a group of detainees almost a year ago, and she remembered how persistently they had been interrogated. Miguel Hidalgo had been alive then, and General Castillo had been in charge. Now there was only Guerrero. Unless she could somehow slip away before she was recognized, she was certain he would kill her.

A little girl in the crowd whimpered.

"Whose child is this?"

"Not mine."

"I don't know. Where's your mother?"

"Are you all by yourself, little one?"

The barrage of questions made the child cry harder, and Elizabeth lifted her into her arms.

"Keep the children quiet!" An officer, threading his way through the crowd, shook a finger at Elizabeth. "The general wants the children quiet."

"Sit down, all of you!"

The gravelly voice pierced Elizabeth's senses, laying her open like a tree struck by a bolt of lightning and exposing her terrorized core to cold fear. She knew that voice well. Along with the others surrounding her, she sat down where she stood, holding the little girl in her lap. Her voice trembled as she buried her face in the child's matted hair and whispered, "Shh, little one. We'll be fine."

"I'm hungry," the girl whined.

"We'll eat soon. We must be very quiet so they'll bring food."

She kept her head down as she watched the tall black boots come toward her. People squirmed to make way, because those boots demanded a path; they would not take the trouble to step over anything. One woman pulled her hand out of their way just in time. The boots were headed straight for Elizabeth. Nausea swirled in her head as she clutched the little girl to her breast.

"I have no time for your petty attempts at trickery," came the guttural warning. "I have no patience with those who take advantage of my generous nature. I gave you a chance."

Oh, God! Staring at the boots, Elizabeth was paralyzed. A blackjack dangled menacingly in the gloved hand that swung near his thigh as he approached. Elizabeth refused to lift her eyes to his terrible face.

The toe of his boot struck her knee as he passed by.

"I assigned a shelter to every area, and I told you to report there by five o'clock. If you're here, it's because you disobeyed that order."

The voice continued to rumble at her back, but it was retreating. The boots were walking away.

"Rations are being distributed at the shelters. You'll get nothing here. Those of you who are charged with looting will find that guilt is easily proved. Think of that while you sit here on your worthless haunches and await my pleasure.''

For several moments Elizabeth could not move. The child in her arms seemed to sense that becoming invisible was necessary for survival, and she, too, sat very still. Finally Elizabeth allowed herself one deep breath, and then another. Suddenly a hand touched her shoulder, and she squeezed her eyes shut and prayed for one more act of deliverance.

''I believe this is the woman, captain. I recognize the scarf.''

Sloan! His deep, rich voice could have been a choir of angels singing. She lifted her head slowly and looked up into gray eyes that lit with joy when he saw her face. ''Yes, this is the one. Please come with me, *señora*.''

He extended his hand, and she laid hers in his warm palm. ''In her confusion she ran from us,'' McQuade explained to the captain. ''Her house was demolished, and most of her family was killed. She's totally disoriented.''

Elizabeth caught his meaningful look and said nothing as she rose to her feet.

''This isn't your child, *señora*,'' he told her as he took the little girl from her arms and handed her to a woman sitting nearby. ''We've found your baby. He's safe.''

She looked at him, and her eyes filled with tears. It was as though fear had left her with a hangover, and she wasn't sure she understood what was being said, but she fastened her hopes on his dear face. McQuade nodded, smiling. "I'll take you to him."

He turned to the captain. "We have her child at the Red Cross office. He's an infant, in need of his mother."

"I can see that this isn't a criminal case," the captain said. "Allow me to escort you to the gate."

As she turned to leave, the little girl called her back with a cry of, "Mama!"

Elizabeth wrenched her whole body toward the cry, but McQuade put his arm around her shoulders and pulled her along. "No, *señora*. This is no time to look back. Your son is waiting."

Tomás! her heart sang. Could he really be telling her that he had located her son? She covered her face with her hands and let her head drop against McQuade's chest as he led her through the crowd. Guerrero could neither see her nor touch her, she thought. She had magic. She had a miracle! She had McQuade.

He flashed his identification at the gate, shook hands with the captain and was hustling Elizabeth across the street when they overheard another announcement from the loudspeaker.

"General Guerrero's son is missing. Male Anglos are to be arrested and brought to the palace for questioning."

The captain turned toward the courtyard long enough for McQuade to duck around the corner, dragging Elizabeth, who had paused in confusion just as the captain had.

"Sloan! Tomás is missing."

"No kidding." Keeping up a steady jog, he switched her hand to his left and pulled the Browning from under his jacket with his right.

"You already have him, then! Where—"

"Shut up, sweetheart, and run like hell!"

They heard shouts behind them, but they didn't look back. Like all small island towns, La Primavera provided a maze of winding back streets. McQuade and Elizabeth soon discovered what the looters already knew: rubble provided good cover. They could only be followed on foot, and their pursuers had gotten a late start.

They hid in a building with a partially collapsed roof until the searchers moved on. Then McQuade led Elizabeth down a dark side street. They were about to dash across the main thoroughfare when a police car came screeching around the corner. McQuade fired two shots, smashing both headlights. The driver put the car in reverse and rapidly disappeared around the same corner.

After they dashed on and took refuge in another alley, McQuade allowed himself a chuckle. "Cop, hell. Felipe's still looking out for number one."

"Sloan, please tell me—"

"Tomás is safe." He glanced back over his shoulder. "You go ahead and let me cover the rear. Hundred-yard dash, honey, all the way to the end of this alley."

Elizabeth hiked up her skirt and let herself go, sailing over all the hurdles in her path. She slowed down when the end of the winding street was in sight, and she turned to find McQuade close behind. He jimmied the lock on the back door of the last shop and ushered her inside.

"I know this place," he explained as he closed the door and locked it. They were both breathing hard. Elizabeth peered into the dark room and realized that it was a bar. "It's always been a cozy port in a storm. Looks like it weathered this one pretty well."

"We're not stopping for a drink, are we?"

McQuade grinned as he flicked the safety on his pistol and tucked it behind his back. "They keep all the good stuff downstairs. Come on."

"McQuade!"

Despite the urge to protest, she followed him through the back room to a basement stairway. It was pitch-dark. She grabbed his arm, and he produced a flashlight. The storage room at the foot of the stairs was filled with liquor boxes, cases of beer, and small, scurrying wildlife. McQuade flashed the light at the unfinished ceiling and disturbed a tiny lizard.

"Hope my buddy, Ed, still keeps his key in the same spot." He found the niche in the floor joist above him and felt around until he sounded a delighted, "Bingo!"

The key opened the lock on another door, which McQuade also secured behind them. Beyond that door was a long passageway filled with kegs and racks of bottles. McQuade gestured with a flourish and announced, "The good stuff."

"Sloan—"

He moved slowly along the passageway, taking careful survey of the racks. "You like really good wine? How about some Château something-or-other?"

"Sloan, where is Tomás?" Elizabeth demanded.

McQuade couldn't suppress his grin. He felt as though he had a great big gift-wrapped box waiting for her under the Christmas tree. "Emilio's got him. Am I a miracle worker, or what?"

"Oh, Sloan." He spread his arms for her, and she went to him gladly. "You are a wonder." She raised her head quickly. "But it's after midnight!"

"And *La Paloma* is on its way to Arco Iris with your son on board. Of course, we're not putting up any signs to advertise the fact." His grin faded as he noted the smudges of fatigue under her bewitching eyes. "What happened, Elizabeth? Why didn't you wait for me?"

She laid her cheek against his shoulder. "I waited forever. I was sure something had gone wrong. Without you there, it was so quiet up on that mountain." She lifted her head again. "Are you sure it was him?"

"Juanita and I found old Maria on the street. I told her I was taking him to the clinic for shots." He laughed, remembering the way Tomás had hung on to him when Dorothy walked into the room. "He's a real cute kid."

She hugged him again. "Now how will we get out of here?"

"I'll think of something. Most of the troops have been pulled back from the village to La Primavera, so

I think we'll head for El Gallo.'' He slid his hand over her bottom. "With me covering the rear.''

"You're outrageous,'' she reminded him.

"Nicest rear I ever covered. Although I oughta paddle it for not staying put.'' She gave him a wary glance. He hastened to add, "But that's pretty far down on my list of priorities of things to do with you.'' The warmth in his smile made her stomach do a cartwheel. He shrugged. "I'd be about as effective at paddling as Felipe is at being a cop. Did you see him gunning the car down the street in reverse?''

"You knew the policeman in that car?''

McQuade laughed. "Yeah, I knew him. *Well.*'' Sobering, he touched her cheek. "Antonio will find us another boat. We'll be out of here before you get fully geared up for a good worry.''

"But so many of the boats were damaged by the storm.''

"He'll find us one. You don't know Antonio.''

She touched his chin in return. "I know you.''

He swallowed, and his voice dropped to an intimate level. "I was scared I wouldn't find you.''

"You should have gone on Emilio's boat with Tomás.''

He shook his head. "No way.''

"If you were with him—'' she laid her hands on his unshaven cheeks and looked into his eyes "—I would know he was safe. I would know...he would have a good life with you. You take your job ser—''

His mouth came down hard on hers, and she rose to meet his kiss with open lips and a welcoming tongue.

He hadn't left her. She indulged herself, rejoicing in that fact. She reveled in the kiss that promised to wipe away fear and pain, and in the touch of hands that would not, *could* not, hurt her. He held the flashlight against her back as he spread his other hand over her bottom and pressed her into him. She arched, rubbing against him like a cat, and he groaned.

"How long can we stay here?" she whispered when he lifted his head. Her pulse pounded, and she was short of breath.

He looked down at her and saw the invitation in her eyes. Her need was as great as his. He closed his eyes and gave his head a quick shake. "We can't stay. We have to get to the village by daybreak."

He moved to put her away from him, but she held him tighter. "Why did we come in here?"

Drawing an unsteady breath, he smoothed her hair back from her temple and kissed her there. "This passage takes us across the street to another bar, owned by the same guy—Ed—" his explanation was punctuated with soft kisses feathered over her forehead "—this guy I know. We're near the edge of town, and, honey, I'm damn near the edge of my sanity."

"I want to know more of you, Sloan." She closed her eyes against the tears that burned to be shed, not from fear, but from a need she'd never experienced before. "If we're caught after we leave here, I never will."

For a moment he just held her. He was afraid to move, afraid to breathe, because the emotion that had suddenly filled him might spill out. Slowly he took her face in his hands and made her look at him.

"Then we can't get caught." His voice was hoarse with feeling, but he managed a smile. "Because when we make love, we're going to take our time, Elizabeth. We're going to get to know each other very, very well."

"You'd made love to me already," she whispered, her throat burning, too. "In a way."

"I can do better than that," he promised. "We'll make it, honey. You have to believe we'll make it." He clearly intended his prophecy to include all the promises for the future it could possibly hold. She closed her eyes and nodded. "Ready for the home stretch?"

"I'm ready."

"That's my girl." With an arm around her shoulders, McQuade led Elizabeth through the dark, bottle-lined passageway. "Ever gone barhopping underground? Some setup, huh? Ed'll have a fit when he finds the door locked and no key around." He gave her a gentle squeeze. "Take it easy, honey. Just take it easy. Don't cry."

Elizabeth dropped her head against his chest as they walked. She let the tears slip silently down her cheeks, amazed that he knew she was crying even in the dark, even though she had made no sound. She had lived in emotional isolation for a long time, but she found that she could keep nothing from this man. And nothing she gave him seemed to turn him against her. Their plane and their boat had both left, and Sloan was still there. She had messed up his plan, but he hadn't gotten angry. He had found her and delivered her from the jaws of her worst nightmare. He was almost too good to be true.

"Here we are," he announced when they reached another door. "Heaven's Gate. I think that's the name of this place." There was another storage room on the far side and, next to it, a stairway. McQuade turned the flashlight off when they reached the top.

"We're only a couple of back streets away from the edge of town." Moonlight from the window drew a halo over the top of Elizabeth's head. Smiling, McQuade touched it. "I don't suppose you've frequented these alleys much."

"I have an idea where we are," she told him.

"There's a little farm on the outskirts near here, and then we hit the boondocks." He peered out the window at the quiet street. "I think we lost 'em. Ready?"

She squeezed his hand. "I'm ready."

They made their way quickly and quietly through the back alleys and ran when they reached a small orchard at the edge of town. Secreting themselves in the tropical underbrush, they doubled back and headed for El Gallo.

Chapter 9

"You should be gone from here, *amigo*." Antonio shook his head in reproach. "Long gone." He hadn't minded being dragged out of bed before dawn—working with private investigators meant being ready for anything—but he'd hoped McQuade had gotten himself and his charges safely off the island by this time.

"Yeah, well, things got a little complicated, and we missed the boat." For Elizabeth's sake, McQuade shrugged off Antonio's concern. She was sitting on the tall stool next to him, looking very tired. "The baby made it, though, and we'll make it the next time."

"It's not so easy now. Their security is tightening." Antonio set three glasses on the bar and brought out a bottle of rum. "I can't sell it, but there's been no directive against giving it away."

"As long as you're giving it away, how about a little bourbon?"

Antonio's laughter rumbled in his chest. "Rum is the drink of the islands, McQuade." He reached for another bottle and set it next to McQuade's glass. "Haven't you gone native by this time?"

Day was dawning, but with the window louvers closed the three were in near darkness. McQuade grinned past the trio of candles that flickered between him and Antonio. "I'll eat your food and...wear your flowered shirts, Antonio, but I won't drink your damned rum."

The line had changed. Antonio remembered it being "eat your food and love your women," and a stronger expletive had usually described the rum. With a chuckle, he glanced at the woman who had induced McQuade to mind his tongue. He knew who she was. There had been much speculation about her exile, and it was the general consensus among the islanders that she had suffered. She had risked her life to return like this. Now the child was safe, and the mother was back in the lion's den.

"They'll start taking the fishing boats out again soon." McQuade poured himself a generous shot of bourbon, thinking he had definitely gotten his days and nights turned around. If he had a sack to hit, he knew he would be out like a light. "They'll have to. These people have to eat."

"Our general is more interested in tight security than in full bellies." Antonio sipped thoughtfully at his rum. "Now that we've lost Castillo and Hidalgo, I think this government will go sour."

"I think it already has."

Elizabeth's quiet statement took both men by surprise. They watched her drain her glass.

"I'll find you a safe place to sleep, *señora*. You need food and rest."

Elizabeth offered a grateful smile, but McQuade raised his palm in refusal. "We'll take the food, but I think we're better off hiding in the jungle, Antonio. And you're better off without us around."

"You think I worry about Guerrero?" Antonio tapped McQuade's shoulder. "You and I are two of a kind, *amigo*. We love to take chances. Besides, you cannot leave here again until nightfall."

The sound of a laboring motor brought the conversation to a halt. Antonio blew out the candles and swept the bottles and glasses from the counter. McQuade glanced at the door to Antonio's living quarters, but decided on the curtain behind the bar. At his signal, Elizabeth slid from the stool. Without a word, they hid behind a stack of boxes. Antonio proceeded to build another stack to enclose them.

The door rattled as someone outside pounded on it, demanding, "Open up!"

McQuade drew his pistol, and Elizabeth listened as the latch was drawn and the door swung open.

heard Antonio come in from the kitchen. "You've got some first aid stuff around here, haven't you, Antonio?"

"Sure, I've got the big, deluxe chest you mount on the wall with the—" Antonio put away the clean glasses he'd brought from the kitchen and came around the end of the bar. McQuade was kneeling by the woman's chair. "Trouble?" Antonio asked.

"Do you have any cold packs?"

"I don't know. I've never let anyone use anything out of my big, deluxe chest."

"Now's your chance, Antonio. Break it out."

"Sloan, I need to lie down," Elizabeth pleaded. He looked up quickly. Her face was becoming chalky even as he watched.

"Good Lord." He came to his feet. "We need a bed, too, Antonio."

"Take mine. Perhaps hot brine..."

McQuade scooped Elizabeth out of the chair and carried her through the door his friend held open for him. "Bring me the whole damned chest, Antonio. Rip it off the wall."

Antonio found the cold packs and hurried after McQuade, hoping his prized emergency kit could stay where it was. "Perhaps a little brandy..."

"Perhaps, perhaps." The bedsprings creaked under McQuade's knee. "Maybe you oughta spray the back room," he grumbled.

"Sloan, please. The man is trying to help us." Elizabeth fought to keep her mind firmly in the present. She felt the chenille bedspread under her palms and saw two bare bulbs in the overhead light fixture. She knew there should only be one, and she concentrated on them until they merged. Something cold was wedged under the knot of pain in her leg.

"Elevate it," Elizabeth suggested. She had a vague notion of a flurry of activity around her, but her own body felt as if it were moving sluggishly through thick air. "Do you think it would be all right...if I slept...just a little while?"

"I don't think I'm going to be able to stop you."

She saw him clearly, his face, looming above hers, softened by a sympathetic smile. She saw herself touch him, saw him kiss her palm, and then she drifted away.

"I don't suppose you've got a doctor around here."

Antonio shifted his gaze from the woman's sleeping face to McQuade's dark scowl. He would have done anything to accommodate this man. One of life's joys was being able to put just the right source or resource at McQuade's disposal. Unfortunately the village had only one healer, and that one would not be to the Anglo's liking.

"There is only *Tía* Teresa."

McQuade sat on the side of the bed and wearily rubbed his hands over his face. "What is she? Some kind of midwife?"

"No." Antonio was hesitant to elaborate. He looked at the woman again. He didn't know what kind of spider had bitten her, but there were poisonous ones on the island. Part of her was of the island, and perhaps that part would connect with *Tía* Teresa's mystical ways. "But she *is* a healer," he attested finally.

"Some kind of folk medicine?"

"I have seen her bring about marvelous cures."

McQuade looked down at Elizabeth and touched the back of his hand to her forehead and cheek. "She's exhausted. Get me some soap and water and some antiseptic. We'll keep the cold packs on her. When she wakes up, we'll ask her if she wants any of that herb stuff."

When McQuade stretched out beside Elizabeth and covered his face with his arms, Antonio took it as his cue to hover elsewhere. He would have to consult with *Tía* Teresa. As a rule she was unwilling to share her curative powers with outsiders. He would have to convince her that Elizabeth was truly an islander and that McQuade was simpatico. He found Chi Chi and instructed her to be on the lookout for soldiers. Taking along the offering of rum the old woman would demand in return for a consultation, Antonio headed for the small house that stood alone at the edge of the village.

McQuade came awake with a start when he was touched decisively, delightfully high on the inside of his thigh. His surprise gave way to a groan of pleasure as he turned to Elizabeth. It disappointed him to discover that she wasn't awake, but disappointment faded as his alarm grew. Her pallid face felt hot and clammy under his hand. He sat up quickly and examined her leg. The cold pack and the pillows he'd propped her leg on had fallen to the floor. Her calf was swollen down to the ankle, the skin stretched taut. He replaced the pillows and applied a fresh cold pack, but beyond that he didn't know what to do.

She moaned.

"Elizabeth? Wake up, honey. We need to talk."

She turned her head aside and moaned again.

McQuade stared for a moment. "You've got to be kidding," he muttered. Filled with an overwhelming sense of helplessness, he sat back on his heels and tipped his head back. "Hey, up there! You've got to be kidding me!" Planting his elbows on the side of the bed, he clenched his fists together and rested his forehead on them. "Now what am I supposed to do? No doctor around, just some superstitious quack, and how in hell can I hide you when you're like this?" He raised his head to look at her again as he knelt beside the bed. "Can't very well stash you behind a pile of boxes in the back room now, can I?" He lifted a long strand of her hair away from her cheek. "If you weren't so damn pretty—"

Antonio knocked as he opened the door and stuck his head in the room. "McQuade, *Tía* Teresa is willing to treat Elizabeth. We'll have to take her over there, though."

"Doesn't she make house calls?"

"House calls?" Antonio selected his words carefully as he came into the room. "McQuade, there is one thing you must understand about *Tía* Teresa. She has no sense of humor. If you try to joke with her, she will be offended."

McQuade sat on the side of the bed. "I'm not feeling very funny, either. We need a doctor, Antonio, not some mumbo jumbo. With my luck, Guerrero's men will come snooping around while this woman is in the middle of some incantation."

"The soldiers would not intrude." McQuade lifted a questioning eyebrow, and Antonio explained, "No one interferes with *Tía* Teresa."

"You mean they wouldn't search her place?"

"No one goes there except for treatment. Her house is inviolate." Antonio shrugged. "Call it superstition, if you will. It's wise not to disturb the sleeping viper."

"Viper! Listen, Antonio—"

Antonio raised his hand against the objections. "The antidote for venom is more of the same."

"You don't think Guerrero's boys want to mess with this lady?" Antonio shook his head. "Let's get her over there, then. I'm not superstitious. I've handled some pretty feisty witches in my time."

As she was lifted into his arms, Elizabeth reached around McQuade's neck. "Sloan?" She reminded him of a sleepy child. "Is it time yet?"

"Relax, honey. I'll get you there. Don't worry about the time."

Unlike most of the older island women McQuade had seen, *Tía* Teresa was thin. Her slightly round-shouldered stance and her frowsy hair gave her the look of a palm tree, with two coconuts slung low on her chest. Her skin was desiccated, like an old piece of fruit. She offered no greeting when she answered the door, but waved the group over her threshold with a long, withered hand.

Turning her back on them, the old woman gestured vaguely toward the back of the house, the papery hand fluttering at the end of her arm. "Put her back there."

McQuade ducked through a curtained doorway, and Antonio followed. The house smelled of balsam and incense. A kerosene flame burned in a red glass lamp in the corner of the room. The bed looked comfortable, and the room was stark but neat. The mattress dipped under McQuade's knee only slightly more than he would have liked as he laid Elizabeth on the bed.

"Leave her to me, now," the old voice said.

"Antonio is leaving, *Tía,* but I'm staying with her."

The old woman scowled first at McQuade, and then at Antonio. Antonio swallowed hard. "This is McQuade, *Tía.* The one I told you about. A man of courage."

Teresa crackled. "More courage than you have, anyway, Antonio. You can't wait to get out of here." She motioned impatiently. "You go out with him," she instructed McQuade. "I'll see to your girl."

"I can't leave her, *Tía.*" McQuade searched for the right excuse. "I made her a promise."

"A promise, you say?" She eyed the sleeping woman and chuckled. "Suit yourself. Maybe you're sick, too. Healthy people usually keep away from me." Taking both men by surprise, she whirled toward Antonio. "Out with you! Go cower somewhere else."

Antonio backed away. "If you need anything, McQuade, just, uh, just send word."

"Paper and pencil," McQuade said quickly. "And ask Juanita if she'll do an errand for me."

After the front door had closed behind Antonio, Teresa went to a cupboard and took out a sheet. "Take her clothes off," she ordered.

McQuade turned to her, surprised. "All of them?"

"Cover her with this," she said, tossing him the sheet. "You might as well be useful. She's fevered. She needs to be sponged. You can help with that."

"Yeah, right," McQuade grumbled in English as the old woman left the room. Stripping off his jacket, he stashed his pistol under the mattress. Then he began with Elizabeth's blouse, lifting her to pull the garment over her head.

McQuade sponged cool water over Elizabeth's face, neck and torso, while Teresa applied a pungent-smelling poultice to the swollen leg. She showed him how to pay particular attention to the backs of their patient's knees and to her underarms, where a little rubbing would release more heat. Together they force-fed Elizabeth a brew of herbal tea, massaging her throat to induce her to swallow. Finally Teresa burned incense, fanning the smoke over the bed while she chanted something in a strange tongue.

McQuade figured the smoke and the chants couldn't do any harm, and he hoped the same went for the woman's other efforts, but he had his doubts about what *good* any of it would accomplish. In light of his doubts, he sat near the lamp and drafted a note on the paper Antonio had sent over.

Dorothy knew every ailment on the island, and she had cures for most of them. McQuade figured she'd been with the Red Cross for almost half a century. His note didn't reveal any names or locations, but he described the problem and asked for medication and instructions. His second request came harder. It was a carefully worded appeal for her to contact Mikal Romanov. He wanted Mike to recover the "canvas bundle" he'd acquired recently and keep it for himself if anything should happen to McQuade and his client. He had told Dorothy that they were headed for Arco Iris when he and Tomás had taken refuge in her back room. Shrouded clues would tell her that only the child was there with the fisherman, Emilio. It was the best provision he could make for little Tomás.

Juanita agreed to deliver McQuade's message and return with the medication. She folded the note into a narrow strip, stitched it into the waistband of her skirt and promised not to take any unnecessary risks. When she returned, she would be carrying first aid supplies for the village.

"It was a brown spider, you say?"

Teresa's question brought McQuade's head around. He'd been watching over Elizabeth from a chair beside the bed and noting that she seemed to be resting more easily since she had drunk the tea. Coming to his feet, he unbuttoned his shirt and reached for the cloth he'd left floating in the basin of water.

"Yeah, brown." He sponged his face and neck, letting the water run freely down his back. "Is that bad?"

The old woman raised her eyebrows as she jerked her chin toward Elizabeth. "For her it was." She stood at the foot of the bed and worked with a mortar and pestle as she talked. "We have many varieties of spiders here. What is important is not the spider's poison, but the victim's susceptibility. Your woman's blood is too thin."

"Oh, yeah?" He glanced at the small cup in Teresa's hands. "Is that some kind of thickener you're working on there?"

"This will attack the poison itself," she explained. "Dried snake."

"Dried snake," he repeated slowly. "What do you do with that?"

"I make a paste of it and apply it to the wound."

"Oh." He nodded as he mopped his chest with cool water, unconcerned about the way it trickled over his belly and into his pants. He was relieved that the old lady didn't have plans to make Elizabeth take the stuff internally.

"It would do no good to feed it to her yet," Teresa added, eyeing McQuade perceptively. "We'll wait until the tea has had some effect."

"Yeah. Good plan." He wondered how long it would take Juanita to get back with some real medication. "What's in the tea?" he asked, plunking the rag back in the basin.

"A blend of herbs."

That sounded harmless enough. He took up his position in the chair again, leaned forward and stroked Elizabeth's damp hair, letting his fingertips linger on her forehead. "How long do you think she'll be like this?" He was willing to give the woman some measure of credit. No doubt she'd seen a great deal in her time.

"Until she recovers or dies." He gave her the look she expected from an Anglo—the fierce denial of the obvious alternatives. In return she offered a cold stare. She would not be accountable to one so ignorant. "Whatever fate decides."

So much for the folk healer, McQuade concluded. Fatalism wasn't to his liking, and he had to make a conscious effort to keep that fact from registering on his face. He would strike a diplomatic balance—trying to avoid offending the old woman while fending off the powdered snake.

"You must leave now," Teresa ordered. "I see that your attitude toward my power is not good."

McQuade straightened his back slowly. "What do you mean not good? I brought her here to get help, didn't I?"

"Since she is one of us I might be able to help her, but not with you watching us."

"I'm not watching you," he said evenly. "I'm watching her. I gave her my word. Now, I don't know anything about this power of yours, but I'm willing to move heaven and hell to see that this woman recovers." He caught the glimmer of surprise in her eyes. "Yeah. Heaven and hell. Which is it, Teresa?"

They glared at each other for a moment, but it was Teresa who backed down and left the room.

McQuade moved to sit on the edge of the bed, needing to be closer to Elizabeth. The tea had had a drugging effect. She was sleeping peacefully, with only the fine mist of perspiration covering her pale skin to betray her illness. Her hair spilled across the white pillow in dark waves, framing her face like an eerie portrait in pallid shades. If she looked otherworldly, there was no question in his mind which world she favored.

"We'll get you through this, angel," he whispered, taking her hands in his. They were cold, and her palms were moist. "The snake powder doesn't sound too promising, but reinforcements are on the way." He took up the cloth from the basin again.

McQuade dozed in the chair next to Elizabeth's bed. The smell of incense and balsam roused him, and the sight of old Teresa waving her palm fan over Elizabeth brought him fully awake. "What's going on?" he grumbled, rubbing a hand over his eyes.

"Be still," Teresa said. "You would not understand. Just watch, and be satisfied that what I'm doing can help her."

McQuade sat up, squinting. The acrid smoke made his eyes burn, but aside from that, he figured it couldn't hurt anyone. Elizabeth turned her head and groaned.

"Have you looked at her leg?" he asked.

"Yes. It's the same."

"Has the swelling gone down any?"

"No, but it's no worse."

"Great." He planted his elbows on his knees and ran his hands through his hair.

"You *should* be grateful. I've seen them swell like a watermelon."

"What happens then?"

"Sometimes they burst." He arched an eyebrow, and she flicked her fingers, spreading her withered hands as she cackled.

"Listen, Teresa, I haven't quite figured out whose side you're on, but I wouldn't be too surprised to find out that you really are a witch." She dropped her hands, her mouth drew up in a tight line, and it was McQuade's turn to chuckle. He tossed the sheet back from Elizabeth's feet and had a look at her leg for himself. Teresa was right; there had been no change.

"Sloan?"

"I'm here, honey." McQuade knelt beside the bed, fussed with the sheet and held her hand. "Feeling any better?"

"I had a bad dream." Her voice was thin and unnaturally high.

"Fever dreams," he confirmed. "They're always bad."

She blinked, trying to bring his face into focus. "Have you had them?"

"Sure." Teresa slipped a fresh basin of water onto the stand next to the bed, and McQuade nodded his thanks. "Are you thirsty?"

"Mmm-hmm."

Teresa took the cue and left the room. Without taking his eyes off Elizabeth, McQuade fished the cloth from the basin, squeezed it out and began bathing her face. It was a service he enjoyed performing, not a task.

"I can't imagine you being sick," she mused in a thick voice. "When was the last time?"

He shrugged. "I don't know. It's been a while."

"Who took care of you?"

"My Aunt Bertie, when I was a kid. And then . . . I took care of myself."

She lifted her hand to his cheek. The gesture felt so tentative that he quickly covered her fingers with his own. "Next time I'll take care of you," she whispered.

Her promise warmed him on the inside like a sip of whiskey. He turned his lips to the center of her palm and kissed her there.

"You need a shave."

He smiled and kissed her again.

"Sloan, I want you to go back to Arco Iris . . . now. Today. I'll come when I'm better." She clasped his hand and pulled it to rest between her breasts. "Please."

"When I go, you're going with me."

She shook her head. "Please, Sloan. For Tomás."

"I haven't forgotten about Tomás." He smoothed her hair back with the damp cloth. "Dorothy will get word to Mike Romanov. I trust him like a brother, Elizabeth. He'll get Tomás to the States, and he and

Morgan will take good care of him until we...until you get back."

Pressing his hand between her breasts, she smiled. "I chose the right man for this job, didn't I?"

"Damn right." Her heart fluttered against his palm, and his throat went dry.

"I want to know that you're safe, Sloan. That Guerrero can't touch you with his hideous, filthy—"

"Shh, shh. He can't touch us, honey." He glanced up at Teresa, who was standing beside him holding a cup. He shifted positions so that he could prop Elizabeth up against his chest. "Look at all we've got going for us," he whispered to her in English. "The Good Witch of El Gallo—*Gracias,* Teresa—and good old Dorothy."

Teresa stepped back and watched the man minister to his woman. She was weak, but she drew on his strength. Antonio had said that the woman was half Anglo and half De Coloran, but she belonged to this man completely. Let him heal her, then, Teresa decided. If she lived, fine; if she died, then it meant his power was not so great. Teresa left the room and returned with a package, which she handed to McQuade.

"Your girl delivered this earlier," she grumbled.

"Juanita?" He set the cup down and lowered Elizabeth to the bed.

"She wanted to give it to you personally, but I scared her away."

Tearing into the package, McQuade found Dorothy's instructions inside a roll of gauze bandaging.

"I scared the soldiers away, too."

He looked up and saw a hint of mischief in Teresa's dark eyes. McQuade grinned. "What the hell's wrong with those guys? Don't they know about the Good Witch of the South?"

Chapter 10

Teresa, if you don't get out of here with that stuff, I'm going to dump this on your head!"

McQuade set the basin aside and peered through the smoky haze at the old woman, who had burned one spice or herb after another over Elizabeth until the room reeked of warring scents. His eyes were teary from it, but *Tía* Teresa stood firm in the midst of it all, glaring at him like a stone gargoyle. With a weary sigh, he snatched his jacket off the back of the chair and pulled his cigarettes from the pocket.

"Hell, you'd probably melt," he grumbled in English. "You make your smoke, I'll make mine." He adjusted his tone of voice to a more civil request in Spanish and came up with an apologetic smile. "Would you stay with her while I take a break?"

"If you think you'll return in a better mood."

He looked down at Elizabeth, whose fitful tossing had ceased for the moment. "Just keep on doing what you're doing," he said. "It seems to be helping."

It was a thinly veiled offer to let the old woman keep up appearances, and he knew she saw through it. It seemed to satisfy her, though, perhaps assuaging her pride. He'd followed Dorothy's instructions and injected Elizabeth with a serum that he prayed would soon take effect. Teresa mumbled continually, and he wasn't sure what she was praying for or, for that matter, to whom she was praying, but he'd decided it didn't much matter as long as she gave them refuge. He'd put his real trust elsewhere.

He flattened his back against the rough stucco next to the front door and watched his stream of smoke dissipate into the night. The cool air felt good on his damp chest. The storm had apparently skirted *Tía* Teresa's little house. There were still blooms on the hibiscus near the front window.

But that back room was hotter than blazes. Heaven and hell, he thought. He'd sworn to move both. He realized that was a pretty brazen claim, but he figured Dorothy might have a little pull with heaven, and heaven might nudge hell aside for Elizabeth's sake. For his part, he could only follow his instincts. Dorothy's note had advised patience. Give the treatment time to work. Patience. Time. *Damn.* He lifted his cigarette to his mouth and drew the smoke deeply into his lungs. He had precious little of either commodity.

"She calls for you again."

McQuade pushed himself away from the wall as he dropped the cigarette and ground it into the dirt. Teresa held the door open for him, and he stepped past her.

Elizabeth looked like a small, wild creature trapped in the untidy thicket of her hair. Her eyes blazed at him when he pushed the curtain aside.

"Get away from me!" she snarled. "I have a gun."

For a moment he thought she might have found his pistol, but his eyes adjusted to the light, and he saw that her hands were empty. He knelt beside the bed and laid his hand on her forehead, easing her head back to the pillow as he whispered, "It's okay, honey. It's Sloan."

"Sloan? I thought you'd gone."

"I just went outside for a smoke." He covered her with the sheet, feeling a little guilty about her appearance. Even when they were living in what amounted to a cave, she'd been perfectly groomed. As soon as he could, he'd fix her hair up for her. "I'm right here," he told her.

"It's too dark." She searched his face as though she weren't convinced of his identity. "Sloan?"

"Yes." He brought her hand to his fuzzy cheek. "Same old Sloan. See? I still haven't shaved."

"Very nice," she whispered, exploring his jaw, his cheekbone, touching his lower lip with her thumb. "The sweetest face. The sweetest, sweetest mouth."

"Shucks," he drawled, smiling. "I'll bet you say that to all the guys you hide out with. Feeling better?"

"I'm very...thirsty."

"Teresa! Bring some tea," he ordered. Then he added, "Please. Not too hot."

Elizabeth grabbed his shoulder with sudden desperation. "Sloan, don't let him take me!"

He saw the wild confusion in her eyes. "Nobody's going to take you from me, Elizabeth." She reached for him, and he caught her against his chest. "You hear me?" He buried his face in the tangled mat of her hair and swore fiercely, "Nobody!"

Her delicate gasp told him that he was squeezing the breath out of her. "I'm okay," she assured him as he settled her back on the bed. "It's strange. Things weave in and out." With a fluttering hand, she described the motion. "Everything seems real, and I'm not sure anything is."

"I'm real. This heat is real." He adjusted the wooden louvers on the small ventilating windows near the ceiling and floor, but it didn't seem to make any difference. Teresa pushed the curtain aside. "Here comes some real tea," McQuade announced, "but I can't vouch for the old lady. She might be mythological."

"I should throw you out of my house and let the vultures have you," Teresa grumbled as she stood waiting for McQuade to adjust Elizabeth against his shoulder.

"Who said *Tía* Teresa lacks a sense of humor?" He grinned as he reached for the cup she'd brought him. He squeezed the old woman's hand and confided, "I think she's better, *Tía*, don't you?"

"We'll see," Teresa muttered, shaking her head as she shuffled out of the room. "We'll see."

"You make damn good tea," McQuade called after her. He held the cup to Elizabeth's lips, and she sipped. "Fit for an island princess," he added as a quiet afterthought.

"You are an impertinent young man," came the answer from beyond the curtain.

McQuade laughed and whispered to Elizabeth, "The woman's crazy about me. Are you jealous?" Elizabeth offered what might pass for a smile and nodded. "Yeah, and you're one sweet old lady," McQuade said, raising his voice so it could be heard in the other room.

"Mind your manners," Teresa snapped back.

"Be careful, Sloan," Elizabeth whispered. "Don't press your luck."

"She's just like the rest of us—likes to be ribbed a little. You don't believe any of that supernatural power stuff, do you?"

"I don't know." She closed her eyes, and her head lolled back against his shoulder. "I believe in darkness and light," she muttered. "When the darkness slides over me... something bad..."

She was drifting again. He laid her back down and turned up the flame on the kerosene lamp. "Teresa, let's get more light in here. Elizabeth hates the dark."

Teresa was accustomed to darkness. Nonetheless her back room now blazed with the light from three lamps. She stood in the doorway and squinted in the brightness at the man and woman who slept peacefully together on the narrow bed. The white sheet was tucked under the woman's arms, covering her breasts, and the man slept in his jeans. He'd combed the woman's hair, taking pains to untangle the dark mane lock by lock with the kind of patience she had thought only a woman could have. Then he'd braided it, washed the woman, washed himself, lain on his belly at the edge of the bed and finally allowed himself some sleep.

One of his arms dragged on the floor and the other guarded the woman. Not from her, Teresa realized. He was an Anglo and was too ignorant to fear her. She was strangely willing to forgive him that. Something in the way he treated her had put a chink in her crusty defenses, and she was willing to let this man get away with his insolence.

He scoffed at the source of her power; she knew that. She was used as a last resort even by those who believed, and then they could never quite look her in the face. They scurried away as soon as they could, and they gave her a wide berth when times were good lest she harm them. This man had brought his woman to her because he feared the soldiers. He trusted her poultice and her tea, but her friends on the dark side were of no consequence to him. She might live to regret it, but she was inclined to allow him his irreverence.

She'd watched him fuss over the woman, harkening to every sound she made, fretting over her pain. The medicine he dispensed might not do any more good than Teresa's herbs. Who could say? They'd used both. What interested Teresa was his power as opposed to her own. She'd beckoned in the darkness, and nothing had happened. It was as though he'd scoffed it all away. So be it, Teresa thought as she watched them sleep. His power was all that was left. Did he think he could love his woman back to health?

If such a thing was possible, she would be glad to let this man accomplish it. Seldom had anyone turned to her with acceptance rather than fear, looked at her and not made her feel repulsive. All his teasing was good-natured, and when he looked at her, he often had a smile on his face.

McQuade caught himself just as he was about to roll off the bed. Cursing, he rolled instead to a sitting position, shielding his eyes with his hands. "What is this, the Super Bowl?" he grumbled. "Who turned on the floodlights?"

"I wondered the same thing."

He twisted around sharply, blinking back the brightness.

"I thought it was probably you." Elizabeth offered him a smile, and her eyes glowed anew.

"Hey..." McQuade's face softened as he returned her smile. "How're you doing?"

"I'm not sure." She tilted her head to look at him from another angle and gave a little laugh. It lacked gusto, McQuade noted, but it was laughter. "Is there really a naked man with very wild hair in bed with me?"

McQuade sat up and stuck his thumb in an empty belt loop. "I've got my pants on, lady. I'm decent!" Laughing, he ran his hand through his unruly thatch of hair. "What you see is what you get."

"Then I must be doing okay." She spoke softly, slowly, as though she hadn't used her voice in a long time. "I think I see an angel."

"Hey, let's not rush it, honey." He took a quick inventory, touching her forehead and her cheek, catching her hand in his. "This is one time I don't mind noticing how much you've cooled off. How's the leg?"

"The one you bit? It still hurts." She lifted a hand to his hair, letting an errant lock tickle her palm. "How long has it been?"

"I lost track." He shrugged. "Couple of days, I guess."

"There's a woman—"

"*Tía* Teresa. Her bark's worse than my bite, but don't let that fool you. She's a good ol' gal."

Her hand slid back to her own shoulder and came to rest on her thick braid. "Who braided my hair?"

"Same old dog who bit you in the leg. How'd I do?"

The tears sprang to her eyes so quickly that she didn't have time to hide them. She could do nothing but wrap her arms around his neck and whisper his name with wonder as she wept.

"That bad?" He held her, half laughing, half wanting to cry himself. "I can fix it, honey. I can do better."

"No, no, no," she said, smiling through her tears. "That good. Sloan, you're that *good*. You took care of me." Leaning back, she took his face in her hands and filled her mind with the sight of his soft gray eyes. "I've never known anyone like you," she whispered.

Her face was lovely and frail and full of tears, and McQuade thought he would burst just from looking at her. He wiped a tear away with his thumb and found just enough voice to tell her, "You gave me a hell of a scare, lady."

"I'll be back on my feet soon. I promise."

"Not unless we get some food in you. Good Lord, you're wasting away." He slid his hand over her shoulder, and the sheet slipped below her breast. That much had not wasted away. He replaced the sheet, but not before her nipple had puckered under his scrutiny. Lifting his gaze to hers, he whispered, "Sorry."

Clutching the sheet, she lay back against the pillow, smiling wistfully.

"Could you eat something?" he pressed.

"I could try."

A desperate squawk silenced them both. A whacking sound drew McQuade's eyebrows down, and when he heard a thud, he had his pistol in his hand. He drew the curtain back. The front door was open, and he saw that it was daylight. There was Teresa, her back to him, with the freshly decapitated carcass of a chicken lying on a stump just outside the door. He could see the neck dangling over the edge.

"Oh, hell, what is she up to now?"

"What is it, Sloan?"

"I don't know, but if she's got any sort of voodoo in mind..." McQuade tucked the pistol at his back as he crossed the front room. He braced his shoulder against the doorjamb. "Teresa, what are you going to do with that poor bird?"

Without turning around, she waved a knife at the ground. "Do you see the head there? Do you see the condition of the entrails?"

"Come on, Teresa, let's not—"

She cut him off with a cackle as she plunked the carcass into a pot of water. "Now the scalding cauldron," she chanted, "makes the feathers fly."

"Teresa, I don't think we need to do anything drastic. Come see for yourself. Elizabeth is—"

"Ha!" She whirled around with more agility than he'd thought possible and held the bird aloft, inches from his nose.

McQuade jumped back before he took a second look. It was plucked. "What the he—"

The old woman's eyes were alight with mischief in a way she rarely shared with anybody. "Now we cook him. Your girl has to eat, doesn't she?"

McQuade's shoulders shook with laughter. *"Bruja,"* he called her. "What a sweetheart of a witch."

While Elizabeth rested in Teresa's care, McQuade searched for a way to get them off the island. Many of the fishing boats were under repair, and most of the fishermen were wary. Guerrero was issuing directives against this and demanding permits for that. No one dared make a move without first getting a military stamp of approval. The village fishermen were an independent breed, but they were still licking their wounds from the hurricane. Word had gotten around, and when they saw Antonio coming, they would shake their heads and wave him back. They shrugged off McQuade's monetary offers with, "Got no place to spend it," or, "Wait a while. Maybe when things settle down."

Discouraged, McQuade sat alone in the cantina, nursing a glass of bourbon and a cigarette. He heard a key rattling in the back door and prepared himself for more bad news from Antonio. But what came was worse. It was Chi Chi in all her buxom glory, and she was moving toward him with a decidedly lascivious grin that made her dark eyes sparkle. Expelling a last lungful of smoke toward the ceiling, he stubbed the butt out in a plastic ashtray.

"What's up, Chi Chi?" McQuade let one foot slide from the rung of the bar stool to the floor and stretched his back. His shirttail was stuffed into his jeans, but the buttons were undone. It was too hot for formality. "What did you do to your hair? It looks...different."

It looked as though she'd washed it in blood, but he wasn't irritable enough to put it quite that bluntly.

Hiking her straight, plum-colored skirt above her knees, she gave herself a boost on a rung on the bar stool next to McQuade's and gradually slid her rump into place on the seat, smiling at him through the whole process. "You like it? It's called Hot and Sassy. I did it for Miami."

McQuade chortled. "I'm sure you'll blow a fuse on their scoreboard, sweetie, if you can just find a way to get there."

With a slow hand she smoothed the skirt over her thigh. "I made myself a new skirt, too. What do you think?"

"Nice." He planted his elbows on the bar and lifted his glass. "Here's to the new Chi Chi."

"*Gracias.* I hope Juanito shares your enthusiasm."

"Juanito?" He could have sworn the act was for him, but he'd been wrong before.

"I call him Juanito because he's just about this tall." The hand she extended indicated a height of less than five feet. She smiled sweetly at the space under her hand, as though a cute little person were standing there. "Not macho like you, McQuade, but still, he's a man, and he's always willing to do *anything* for me."

"Oh, yeah?" McQuade sipped his bourbon. "Is he a Miami fan, too?"

"He has a boat."

McQuade slid his gaze her way and smiled. "Oh, yeah?"

"Oh, yes, McQuade." She propped herself prettily on the bar and posed with a pout, eyeing the dusting of light hair on McQuade's bronzed chest. "Little Juan has a big boat. Big enough to take you and me and that scrawny friend of yours all the way to Miami."

Swiveling on the stool, he faced her as he set his glass down. "What will it cost me for tickets to this cruise?"

She slid to the floor and stepped closer. "I believe the polite question is what will it cost *me*?"

"Well, look—" The hand she slipped inside his shirt was bad enough, but the one on his thigh reminded him of the need he'd felt for Elizabeth in recent days. "How about we work a trade?"

Chi Chi lowered her lashes and smiled. "Mmm-hmm?"

"I've got season tickets to the Dolphins' games."

The smile became a scowl. "Do you think some football player with fake shoulders and a thick neck could take the place of the man of my dreams?"

"You mean Juanito?"

McQuade took a not-so-playful fist in the breast-bone. "I don't have to introduce you to my friend, McQuade."

She'd managed to slip the strap of her skimpy blouse off her shoulder. McQuade smiled as he slowly slid it back into place. "How soon can you arrange it?"

"I'm seeing Juanito this afternoon. We can meet you here around nine."

"I'll be here," he promised.

She snaked her hand behind his neck. "You can make your plans, and then Juanito will go back to get his boat ready. And then you and I . . ." Craning her neck, Chi Chi pressed her mouth against McQuade's.

His body responded because she was female, and Lord knew he'd been hungry for one. But not this one. His brain clicked into autopilot as he went through the motions of kissing Chi Chi. He wanted Elizabeth. More than that, he wanted Elizabeth *safe*, and he'd do whatever he had to do to see to it. Even this. Even more than this. The thought occurred to him that when he'd used women for himself it had never bothered him. But the idea of using anyone for Elizabeth's sake made him hurt inside.

McQuade wiped the back of his hand across his mouth as he walked back to Teresa's house. A couple of kisses had left his lips feeling gritty. The sky was clouding over, and he hoped it would rain right now and get it over with. Since it didn't, he went to the side of the house and filled the metal tub with rainwater from the cistern. Stripping to the waist, he gave himself a bath.

He found Teresa preparing to go out. He hadn't known her to leave her yard before, but she seemed anxious to be gone and impatient with him for dawdling in the water and letting his hair drip on her floor.

"Do you think I've got nothing better to do than tend to this woman?" she grumbled. "She thinks she's well enough to wash clothes and meddle in my kitchen, and I've had all I could do to keep her in bed this morning. That should be your job."

He almost missed the twinkle of mischief in Teresa's eyes. "Yeah, well..." He grinned when he caught it. "Maybe someday. You think she could travel pretty soon?"

"I thought that would be the next thing on your mind. She's as frail as a newborn."

"We've gotta get out while the getting is good, and you just said she was trying to—" He frowned. Teresa had hung several bags made of woven sisal over her arm, and she was tying a scarf over her frowsy hair. "Where do you think you're going, old lady? It's going to rain."

"It rains often, but I have things to do."

"Like what?"

"That woman drinks my tea, uses everything in the house. I have to make a new collection." She pointed to the top of her cupboard. "Hand me that bottle."

"How long do you think you'll be gone?" He took the bottle down and gave it to her. "I'm telling you, it's going to rain."

"You'll be gone tomorrow, won't you?" she asked.

"Probably, if things work out."

"I won't be here. But you must take some of that—" she pointed to a jar on the shelf "—and make her tea twice a day. And that's the salve for her leg. You know what to do with it."

"What do you need more stuff for now?" McQuade demanded. "You're going to be out there in the jungle all night?"

Ignoring his bluster, she handed him the bottle. "This is witch hazel."

Snatching the tall glass container, he gave it a disdainful once-over. "What, you've got her in a bottle?'' He offered Teresa a teasing grin. "I suppose she's your sister."

"Your impertinence will bring you to no good end, young man. You use this on that woman."

"That woman's name is Elizabeth."

Teresa looked up at him, her eyes dancing. "She's a pretty little thing, too. You rub this on her back. She's been lying in bed too long. This will make her skin tingle."

"Oh yeah?" McQuade chuckled as he took another look at the bottle. "Why, you sly old—"

"You do your job now." She poked him in the chest and fluttered her hand toward the back room. "I have to be about my business." When she actually smiled, McQuade thought he saw the young woman Teresa must once have been. "Your power has been good for her," she confessed. "Better than mine. Go on now. Take care of her. Let her take care of you."

McQuade heard the door close quietly behind her as he drew the curtain aside.

Elizabeth was lying fully dressed on the bed, and she reminded him of a child who'd fallen asleep waiting for someone to come and take her somewhere. He hoped he'd be able to take her somewhere soon, but he didn't want to get her hopes up until he had a firm offer. Her bare feet peeked at him from under the hem of her full yellow skirt. Like a swatch of black silk, her braid fell across the front of her white peasant blouse. Sitting at the edge of the bed, he laid a possessive hand on her hip, and she stirred lazily.

"Hi." McQuade smiled as she rolled over on her back and blinked at him. "Dressed for a date?"

"I hope so. Do we have one?"

"I'll check my calendar." He drew the bottle from behind his back and held it up in front of her. The clear liquid inside reflected the light from the lamp that burned near the foot of the bed. "Do you know what this is?"

"If you're drinking it, it must be bourbon," she guessed. She sat up and scooted back, clasping her arms around her knees. "And if we're having a party, I'm ready. I'm going crazy."

"Feeling frisky, are we? Teresa said you were trying to overdo it today."

"Teresa wouldn't allow me to do anything," she informed him. "I was fortunate to be able to bathe myself and wash my hair."

"You would have been more fortunate if you'd waited and allowed me to do that. But never mind." He took the cap off the bottle and sniffed. "Hmm."

Elizabeth leaned forward and took her turn. "Let me guess. It's one of Teresa's brews."

He snapped his fingers. "Right you are. Guaranteed to make the lady's skin tingle and her toes curl. I have the witch doctor's instructions to rub this stuff—" he slid her a crooked smile and relished each word "—all over your body."

Elizabeth laughed, and the sound came from deep in her throat. "Witch hazel, I'll bet. Where's Teresa?"

"She rode off on her broom." Cocking a teasing eyebrow, he raised his forefinger. "But I heard her exclaim as she rode out of sight, 'Make her happy, McQuade.'"

Elizabeth's smile faded, and her dark, trusting eyes met his. "We're alone, then?" He nodded. "And she actually said that?"

"Words to that effect." He was no longer smiling. His voice turned husky. "Turn over on your stomach. I'll start with your back."

"No. Not my back."

She lowered her eyes and would have retreated if it had been possible, but he wouldn't allow it. He set the bottle on the table beside the bed. "Your back," he said firmly, "is as beautiful as your front, and, believe me, I'm qualified to make that statement."

He saw the signs of capitulation as he persuaded her with gentle hands to lie down again. It wasn't what he wanted, but it was the only response she knew. Today he would teach her another one.

She lay facedown on the bed and thought of all the care he'd taken with her, all the tenderness he'd shown, and she knew he wouldn't hurt her. This was Sloan. She would be still for him.

He sat at the edge of the bed, moved her braid aside and slipped her blouse over her shoulders. The flat bones in her back protruded at odd angles as the muscles around them tensed, but she made no move to stop him from pushing the blouse to her waist. He took some of the liquid in his hand and began smoothing it over her shoulders. His palms tingled with it.

"I think we've got a good thing going here," he decided. "How does it feel?"

"Good," she said tightly.

"That's all I've got in mind." His hands moved in small circles, and he spoke to her quietly. "I just want to make you feel good."

"Sloan..."

"I used to wonder why my mother left me and never came back," he told her, his soft, rich voice stroking her even as his hands did. "I used to worry about it. Was it because she didn't like me? I wondered if it showed, if I affected other people the same way, if they could tell by looking at me that my own mother didn't want me."

He felt some of the tension dissolve under his hands. She opened her eyes and concentrated on the empty chair next to the bed, and her thoughts turned from herself. "I don't know why she did what she did, but I know it had nothing to do with you," she said. "Looking at you, I see only beauty and...and kindness."

He chuckled. "You saw that from the very first, did you?"

There was some hesitation. "No. Not the first night."

"Nor even the day after that, right?"

The cooling witch hazel made her tingle under the warmth of his caressing hands, and she relaxed more. "I see it now," she told him. "That's what matters."

The caresses moved to her lower back, and then he pushed her skirt below her waist, and his hands stilled. Elizabeth couldn't draw breath. She knew what he was seeing. His lips touched the place just above the swell of her hip, the only physical mark of her shame, and she squeezed her eyes shut.

"I saw this the other night when I was bathing you," he told her. There was no hint of shock in his voice, no horror. His kiss was like a touch of satin against her, and his breath warmed the cold, white mark. "It made me angry, but I'm glad you didn't see that. You might have thought the scar itself displeased me."

"It's an ugly thing." Her voice was small and thin, and the pain in it pierced him.

"What he did was an ugly thing, and my anger was for him, and for myself for not being there to stop him."

"But you didn't know me then."

"I do now. That's what matters." He kissed her again, and he heard a trembling intake of breath fill the hollow, lonely places inside her. He wanted to fill those places with something warmer, and this was where it would start. With a deep, cleansing breath. "I don't know why he did what he did, Elizabeth, but it had nothing to do with you."

He peeled her clothes away, sliding them over her legs, and he stroked her back and her buttocks, telling her over and over how beautiful she was. She turned to him, her eyes brimming bright with tears, arms reaching for him. He slid over her and covered her mouth with his. She dropped her head back and drank in his kiss, letting his tongue have access to the soft, moist cavern of her mouth. When he raised his head, the tears had slid from the corners of her eyes, and her lashes glistened.

"You're the *most* beautiful," she said, smiling up at him.

"Not from where I'm sitting."

"I wish—"

"Shh, don't tell me what you wish." He touched the damp spot where the tear had trailed into her hair. "I can't change the past. Tell me what you want right now."

"I hardly know." And that truth frightened her, too.

"Then trust me. Let me give you something new."

He kissed her, made her mouth soft, and moved his lips over her neck and her breasts, testing her as he tasted her. If she seemed to hesitate, his touch became tentative, teasing her until she thrust her breast into his palm and filled his mouth with her tongue. He groaned and pulled her body against his, so that she would know how it was with him, and how much of him he was asking her to trust. In answer, she drew his head back to her breast and invited him to suckle her. It was her turn to give, and he took satisfaction as he gave breathtaking delight.

When he kissed her mouth again there was a gathering of heat between them, a systematic building of energy, one impulse exciting another. She writhed against him, holding him, exploring, finding the button at the top of his jeans and tugging it loose.

"Elizabeth?" he whispered.

"You're what I want, Sloan."

"Are you sure?" He slipped his hand between them and caressed her on the soft curve of her inner thigh. He knew damn well it was an unfair question, but he was past the point of being fair. He'd settle for being the best thing that had ever happened to her if she'd just say...

"Oh, Sloan..."

He touched her and found a readiness that made him harder than he had been. She arched her back, surging into his hand, and he touched her again.

"Please, Sloan. Make love to me."

He unzipped his pants, and she slid her hands over his hard, smooth buttocks. Growling, he shucked the jeans in one quick movement and knelt between her thighs, bracing himself over her on unsteady arms. She reached for him, held his hips in both her hands, and he came nearer to her cautiously, by slow degrees. She gasped as she felt him fill her.

"Is it okay?" he asked.

He knew it was. He could see it in her face, but he wanted to hear her say...

"Yes."

He moved inside her, slowly.

"Oh, yes!" This was Sloan, and she couldn't be still. She remembered the swing, the way he had pushed and she had flown, and she said, "Yes, Sloan, yes."

He slid deeper inside her, and then he remembered the swing, too, and he whispered, "How much higher, honey?"

She raised her knees—higher—lifted her hips—still higher. "Oh, Sloan—as high as we can go!"

McQuade held her until she went to sleep. Then he slipped out of bed, pulled his jeans back on, and made them some supper. After they'd eaten, they made love again, and then they lay in each other's arms and listened to the rain pinging softly on the corrugated metal roof.

He'd unbraided her hair, and he sifted his fingers through it, letting it fall like corn silk against his arm. "I have to meet some guy over at the cantina in a little while," he said hesitantly. "I'll be back just as soon as I can."

"Does this guy have a boat?" Elizabeth asked, trying not to sound too hopeful. She knew that, if he did, Sloan had kept that information from her for a reason.

"He's supposed to. We'll see." With a sigh, he dropped his head back to the pillow and stared at the ceiling. "He's a friend of Chi Chi's, and Chi Chi's kind of...spacey. You never know."

"But you are the man of her dreams," Elizabeth teased as she toyed with the springy hair on his chest.

"Yeah, well, this guy's supposed to be sort of a boyfriend, so I guess I've been replaced." He kissed the top of her head. "You'll be okay for an hour or so?"

"Of course." She pulled his head down and stretched her neck to offer him a reassuring kiss, running her hand along the growth on his cheek that was fast becoming a beard.

He groaned with pleasure. "Do me one more favor."

"What?"

"Say my name again."

She nuzzled his neck and said it softly, deep in her throat. "Sloan."

He smiled at the sound. "You're the only one who calls me that anymore."

"Does anyone else even know it's your name?"

"I don't think anyone else ever asked." Wrapping her in his arms, he drew her close for another moment. He didn't like the idea of leaving her to go out in the rain.

He liked the idea of meeting Chi Chi at the cantina even less.

Chapter 11

Guerrero's directive was posted on the cantina door.

Liquor sales prohibited. Martial law has been declared during this state of emergency by order of General Rodolfo Guerrero. Violators will answer charges before the military tribunal.

McQuade stared at the stamped signature and considered what he would give for ten minutes alone with its owner. No hardware, no witnesses. Just one-on-one.

The louver in the window was lifted, and an eyeball appeared in the crack. A stage whisper followed. "Come to the back door."

McQuade played along. He hadn't walked up to the front door without checking around the premises first, but Antonio's game had its rules. Somewhat to McQuade's surprise, it was Chi Chi who led him through the tiny kitchen and past the bedroom, where a kerosene lamp burned beside the bed.

"My father is out," she whispered, smiling. "He probably won't be back tonight."

It occurred to him that that kind of smile wasn't as attractive to him as it once had been. "Is your friend here?" he asked.

"Just as I promised." She took his forearm in both hands and pressed her finger gently downwards, as though testing a piece of fruit for its ripeness. "And I heard my father say that he's been planting a story about a certain child who's missing. Some clever Anglo made off with the boy in a little Beechcraft airplane. You have nothing to worry about, McQuade." The lambent look she flashed told McQuade otherwise. "We are looking after you very, very well."

Juanito waited in the corner of the cantina, where one candle provided a dim circle of light on the low ceiling above the little wooden table. He was a short man, but he had the beefy shoulders of a net-hauler. He greeted McQuade with a hearty handshake and the kind of straightforward attitude that gave McQuade a pang of regret. Juanito was getting a line from Chi Chi, and McQuade had to feed into that, at least initially. If he cooperated completely, though, Juanito would be well paid.

McQuade returned the friendly grin and cast a meaningful glance at Chi Chi. Island custom excluded women when the men sat down to talk. "You ready to talk business, *amigo*?"

Chi Chi looked from one man's face to the other, posturing with her hands at her hips. "Going to Miami is my business. *You* said you'd get me across the water." She pointed a red fingernail at Juanito's head, then turned it on McQuade. "And *you* will get me into the city. Just so you know." She turned on her heel and marched behind the bar. "I'll get you drinks, but I'll be listening to every word. That's the way they do it in Miami, you know."

Juanito chuckled. "I like a little fire in a woman. Don't you, *señor*?" Leaning over the table, he added from behind his cupped hand, "But this one is some big handful, if you know what I mean."

"I think I can sympathize." McQuade pulled out a pack of cigarettes and offered one to Juanito. "You've got a boat that can get us as far as Key West?"

"Miami!"

"We'll drive to Miami, Chi Chi." McQuade lit Juanito's cigarette, then held the match to his own. "The woman who's with me has been sick. I need to get her out of here as soon as possible."

Smoke swirled around Juanito's head. "I was fortunate to have been in Arco Iris when the storm hit. My boat wasn't damaged. But these are troubled times, *señor*."

"And transportation is at a premium," McQuade finished for him. "I'm well aware of that. What's your price?"

"Five thousand American dollars."

Hell of a bargain, McQuade thought, but he didn't let the thought register on his face. "You got a crew?"

"My son and I can handle the boat."

Damn. Another kid. "How old's your son?"

"Eighteen. And big for his age." Juanito held his hand several inches above his own head.

McQuade smiled. "Look, we're running a risk here. If you want to leave your son out of it, I can crew for you."

"Just being alive in these times is risky. We have taken chances before." He gave a conspiratorial wink. "You are not the first to come to this island, or leave it without going through the port authority."

Chi Chi delivered three drinks to the table and lifted her glass with a cheerleader's enthusiasm. "Here's to Miami, where all the action is!"

As Chi Chi had planned, Juanito left soon after her toast to prepare his boat for an early morning departure, but she hadn't planned for McQuade to leave with him, in the interest of scouting things out. It was disappointing to be left alone to blow out her lamp and wait until it was time for her to go down to the dock. Her only consolation was the promise of big city lights to come—the kind she would never have to blow out.

* * *

Elizabeth sat in the chair by the bed and waited. Every sixty seconds made a minute, every sixty minutes made an hour, and every sound outside made her lose count. Waiting alone in the house took every ounce of control she had. McQuade's face in the doorway was the most beautiful sight imaginable. She came out of the chair like a shot and fell into his arms.

"Hey, I'd say we're recovering nicely." He basked in the warmth of a smile that suggested nothing but joy at his return.

"I waited, Sloan. It seemed like forever, and I thought I heard . . . I don't know what I heard, but I waited."

"You did fine, honey." Far from patronizing her, he was proud. He rubbed her back affectionately. "This is a spooky place. How's the leg?"

"It itches."

"Can you walk on it?" She nodded hopefully. "What do you say we blow this joint, then?"

"Chi Chi's friend will take us?"

"Chi Chi came through. And according to her, word's out that Guerrero's son was kidnapped by an Anglo, who managed to fly him out of here in a single-engine Beechcraft."

"But that's . . ."

McQuade smiled. "Antonio has a wonderful way with rumors."

"So they're not looking for us?"

"I think Guerrero's got his hands full keeping order in the city. If we can get by the patrol boats, we should be okay.'' He hesitated. ''And then there's Chi Chi.''

''Chi Chi?''

McQuade took Elizabeth's flowered scarf from the bedside table and draped it over her head. ''Chi Chi's going to have to miss the boat again,'' he said as he tied the scarf under Elizabeth's chin. Wrapping her in his jacket, he added, ''There's no way I could get that woman past customs. Besides, Miami has enough problems.''

Juanito was waiting for them at the dock. Wordlessly they followed him past the boats in various states of disrepair that bobbed in the water like so much flotsam. Gentle waves slapped against the hulls and washed ashore, and worn wood creaked with the motion. It was a warm night, with a slip of a new silver moon brightening the starry sky.

The agile little fisherman hopped onto the deck of his boat and lifted his brawny arms as McQuade handed Elizabeth down to him. ''I have a place below where you can rest,'' Juanito told her. ''We'll be on our way soon.'' He gestured to the lanky young man who had apparently been sleeping in a chair on the deck. ''This is my son, whose name is also Juan.'' The boy rose obediently and dropped the army blanket he'd been wrapped in back on the chair. He stood more than a head taller than his father. Juanito clapped a hand on his son's back. ''I guess he'll be Big Juan, and I'll be Little Juan, right? This way,'' he invited, and Elizabeth followed him below deck with McQuade in tow.

Once she was settled, McQuade followed Juanito up to the wheelhouse.

"If we get stopped, there is a compartment right here—" Juanito popped open a door that blended in with the woodwork just below the wheel "—that hides a man quite nicely. We'll just say the woman came along with my son, and Chi Chi—" He checked his watch. "Chi Chi is holding us up." Frowning, he peered through the window toward the dock.

"Chi Chi is under the impression that she has another hour or so to get her act together." McQuade positioned himself carefully between Juanito and the door. "I'm afraid Chi Chi's not going to make this trip."

"Oh, but this was Chi Chi's idea. She'll be very—"

Juanito turned and found McQuade's pistol pointed at his belly. "Tell Juan to cast off," McQuade said quietly.

He was glad Elizabeth wasn't there to see him pull a gun on this man. Juanito's eyes bulged as he glanced up at McQuade's face and then in his son's direction. He swallowed convulsively, without quite closing his mouth, then cleared his throat and called out to the boy. "Let's cast off, Juan, while the coast looks clear."

Young Juan complied without comment. The engine rumbled, and the small fishing craft pulled away from its mooring, leaving the village of El Gallo in its wake. The boy went back to his deck chair, trusting his father's judgment as the boat churned through the inky water in search of open sea. McQuade didn't like himself much for giving the idea that the boy was part of an insurance package, but he had to consider Elizabeth first.

Juanito maneuvered across the little harbor. If they were stopped, it would happen near the channel, a fact which was on the minds of both men as they scanned the horizon.

McQuade was so absorbed in his act of piracy that Elizabeth's voice gave him a start.

"What's happened, Sloan?" McQuade's head came around only long enough to catch the look in her eyes. It wasn't one he wanted to deal with just then, and he turned his attention back to Juanito.

"Nothing, honey. We're on our way."

"What has this man done?" Her voice betrayed confusion and disbelief.

"He's left his girlfriend behind."

"But why the gun?" Elizabeth insisted.

"Saves questions," McQuade offered. "Simplifies matters, and gets us on our way. We're not going to Key West, Juanito. We're headed for Arco Iris."

Juanito shrugged. "That's fine with me. It's closer."

"It wouldn't have been fine with Chi Chi."

Juanito lifted his eyebrows in assent. "Chi Chi could almost smell Miami this time. Me? I like the smell of the islands better. I took this job for the money, *señor*, not for Chi Chi."

"Oh, yeah?"

"Please, Sloan," Elizabeth entreated. "I think we can trust this man. No more guns."

"Understand me, Juanito. This woman has a little boy waiting for her in Arco Iris. I intend to see that she gets there."

"I have a son, too, *señor*."

"Yeah." Somewhat chagrined, McQuade put his weapon away. "There was no way in hell I was taking Chi Chi to Miami," he mumbled as he fished in the breast pocket of his shirt for a cigarette.

"She's probably pacing the length of the dock right about now." Juanito's laugh was hesitant at first as he allowed himself to relax a little. Then he pictured what he'd described, glanced at McQuade's empty gun hand and laughed again. "I can always tell her you held a gun on me. But you, *señor...*"

The man's laughter was contagious, and McQuade couldn't resist. "God help me if that woman ever does find a way to get to Miami." He offered Juanito a cigarette.

Juan's lean face appeared in the doorway. "Patrol boat coming, Papa."

McQuade moved away from the window and nodded at Juanito to take a look. Juanito confirmed the news. "I can't outrun them. That's our best bet." He indicated the compartment he'd shown McQuade earlier.

McQuade allowed himself a glance at Elizabeth. She braced herself visibly and smiled as she lifted a hand to touch his bearded cheek. He took her hand to warm it in his and shifted his glance to Juanito. All the advice he'd given Elizabeth about trust came back to haunt him. Trust *me* had been easy to say. Trust her life to the good graces of some fisherman he'd just met? It was almost unthinkable.

"Don't make any mistakes." McQuade shoved the cigarettes back in his pocket as he riveted Juanito to the deck with a cold stare. "If anything happens to her, Juanito, I'll get you before they get me. I promise you that."

"Sloan." The sound of her voice softened him inside, and when he looked at her, his fear showed. "That's not the way," she said quietly.

He lifted the scarf, which had slipped to her shoulders, and tied it over her head. "You've had a fever," he reminded her.

"I'll be all right."

"She will if you get out of sight, *señor*." Scowling, Juanito jerked his chin toward the compartment again.

As the cruiser approached, its searchlight flooding the deck of the fishing boat, Juanito cut the engine. Elizabeth joined Juan on deck. She had her role to play. Juanito had given her a pair of shapeless paints that she'd rolled to mid-calf, a faded sweatshirt with a hood and a pair of canvas deck shoes. With her thick braid tucked inside the sweatshirt and the scarf over her head, her identity, her age, even her sex, became almost indeterminate.

"Getting an early start?" The voice from the cruiser echoed through a bullhorn.

"Yes, sir," Juan called out. He took the cue to drape a protective arm around Elizabeth's shoulders as Juanito appeared on deck.

"Not much competition for territory these days," the voice said. "Everybody else is beached."

"Getting a jump on those Mexicans from Arco Iris," Juanito shouted back. "People have to eat."

"Papers in order?"

"You see my tags."

A beam of light flashed over the bow of the fishing boat, where the evidence of his registration was fastened.

"Just you and your kids?"

"My son and his betrothed. Pretty hard to put together a crew lately."

"Forecast looks good for today. Save us a nice piece of marlin."

The three stood silently, bracing themselves as the little fishing boat rolled over the retreating cruiser's wake.

"I owe you, Juanito." McQuade came down the steps from the wheelhouse. "Starting with an apology."

The edge of the world lightened gradually with the promise of a new day. McQuade braced his forearms on the railing and looked out over the stern at the horizon. He took a final deep drag from his last cigarette. Then he flicked it overboard and watched it arc high before hitting the water. The sun was coming up, and they were nearly home free. Elizabeth had said nothing to him since the patrol boat had given them a reprieve.

She would have Tomás back soon, and then hadn't she once said she'd be moving to New England? He figured the five thousand he owed Juanito would take the rest of his advance, since he'd already given Emilio five thousand. Realistically the trip hadn't cost him much except his time, and he could afford that. They were getting down to the wire, and it was time to take an objective look at himself and the emotional vise he'd willingly put himself into.

He felt her beside him before he turned to see her there. The scarf had slipped from her head again. Even the oversize clothes could do nothing to diminish the dignity in her bearing. McQuade decided he wouldn't take any final tallies of what this trip had cost him until she said goodbye.

"Do you have another cigarette?" she asked.

He shook his head. "Fresh out."

"Too bad." She shrugged, shoved her hands into her pockets and leaned against the rail. "I had a sudden craving."

"Just as well I ran out. You should be resting."

She shook her head, letting the wind take the loose wisps of hair away from her face. "I can't take any more cramped quarters. Besides, I wanted to watch the sun rise on this day."

He'd been watching the pink streaks gather above the calm sea, gaining in intensity like a musical prelude. "It's going to be a beauty, all right."

"I know you did what you felt you had to do," she said quietly as she gazed out at the sea. "But seeing you hold a gun on that man . . ."

"I've been carrying it since the first day, Elizabeth. I use it when I have to."

"But he wasn't threatening us. For a moment I was on his side and not—"

"Not on mine. I noticed."

"He had agreed to help us."

"He'd agreed on certain terms, and I changed the terms. When you don't have time to argue, you play your ace. It's as simple as that."

McQuade straightened, held the rail in both hands and drank cool air from the salty rim of morning. He didn't feel clean, but he told himself that all he needed was a shower and a shave, and he'd be fine.

"Would you have shot that man?" she asked him finally.

He gave her a long, hooded look. "I don't pull a gun on a man unless I'm willing to use it. I know it, and I make sure he knows it. Nine times out of ten, that's all it takes."

"You mean the threat is usually enough."

"That's right." Folding his arms across his chest, he turned to face her. "Why did you hire me, Elizabeth? Remember all those qualifications you thought I had? You could handle the gun yourself. I showed you how—remember? But you didn't know if you could use it." He tapped his fingertips against his own chest. "You hired me because that's what I do. When the chips are down, all the channels are exhausted and everybody's hands are tied, people come to me because I'm willing to use the gun if I have to."

"But with Juanito—"

"I couldn't be sure, and I didn't have much time. There are no superheroes, Elizabeth. You wanted the Lone Ranger? Well, all you got was me." He knew what she was thinking. How were his tactics any better than Guerrero's? She would have to sort that out for herself, he decided. "Anyway, we're headed for Arco Iris, and your kid's waiting there for you."

She turned her face toward the rising sun and smiled. "So the day begins."

"So you have arrived, my friends." Juanito watched his son tie the boat to a piling. He turned to McQuade and cocked his hands on his hips. "You are safe. I am still alive, since you found no fault with my services. When I see Chi Chi again, well..." He shrugged and gave his head a dramatic shake. "That condition may change."

McQuade laughed. "Take her a present, *amigo*. You've got a bonus coming. Fix her up with something sparkly and she'll probably let you off easy." Sobering, McQuade offered his hand. "We owe you our lives, Juanito. I only did what I did because—"

Juanito accepted the handshake with a broad grin as he glanced at Elizabeth. "I know. For this lady, I would have done the same."

"Thank you, Juanito," she said.

"I will see you with your son before I leave here, *señora*," he said. "I have thought of nothing else all day long—to see the happiness on your face."

"Yes." An irrepressible smile burnished her dark eyes. "Yes, you will. As soon as I—Sloan . . ."

"The first thing we do is get to the Oyster Shell, so I can take care of Juanito, get cleaned up and find out where Emilio lives," McQuade said. "I'll meet you there later, Juanito. First round's on me."

McQuade reached for Elizabeth's hand. He felt the tremors of excitement ripple through her body as he helped her plant her feet firmly on the weathered boards of the pier. The slanted rays of late afternoon sunshine were still warm, and the lush green, lazy little island basked in them. McQuade slung his jacket over his shoulder and fixed his mind on a long drink and a large, rare steak. The idea reached his stomach, which seconded the motion with an audible growl.

Elizabeth favored her injured leg as she tried to set a faster pace than she could handle. "I can't wait for you to do all that," she complained.

"And I'm going to get a doctor to take a look at that leg."

"After we get Tomás. Oh, Sloan, do you think he'll remember me?" She looked down at her skirt, then grabbed her braid and examined that, too. "Maybe a shower and some clean clothes."

"Might not be a bad idea." He slid her a loaded glance. "They say a mother's scent is the first thing her child learns to recognize."

"McQuade! Are you saying I might . . . smell?"

He laughed. "Not to me, lady. We've been hanging out in the same rat holes." He watched her adjust the scarf, which had slipped to her shoulders again. For once she looked a little disconcerted, her dignity bruised, and he took a perverse enjoyment in that look.

Felix Santiago was overjoyed when the two bedraggled guests presented themselves at the desk in the lobby of the Oyster Shell.

"McQuade, my friend! I was beginning to wonder whether you'd be back to pay your bill. I've been holding your rooms. At ninety dollars each a night, that's—"

"That's a hell of a way to greet an old friend," McQuade interrupted. They shared a laugh and pumped each other's hands.

"Emilio Gomez had a harrowing story to tell," Felix said as he handed two keys over the desk. "We were afraid we'd have to count you among the missing at De Colores."

"Is Tomás all right?" Elizabeth asked anxiously.

"The child?" Felix smiled. "He's fine. You might have some trouble separating him from the Gomezes, though. They've become quite attached."

"I left a few things in the room, Felix. Are they still there?" she asked as she edged toward the stairs.

"Everything is as you left it," Felix assured her. He turned to McQuade. "What can I get you, my friend?"

Watching her push herself up the steps purely on adrenaline, McQuade decided to postpone the drink and the steak. "How about a razor?"

McQuade walked Elizabeth to the Gomez home. It meant climbing a hill, and he fought the urge to lift her into his arms and carry her along the gravel path. A chunk of wood or a flat rock served as a step every few yards. When at one steep spot she bent over, seeking a rock for a handhold, he gave up the fight and swept her off the ground.

"Sloan, no, I can..."

He made an effort to sound matter-of-fact, to look into her eyes without betraying himself. "Elizabeth, I won't have you crawling up this hill."

"It looks outrageous, but I guess we're beyond that," she admitted as she settled her arm around his shoulders.

"No kidding," he said drily and proceeded up the hill.

The little house overlooked the bay. From it, Emilio could keep an eye out for his boat, the weather and the temperament of the sea. When they arrived, Luisa Gomez was taking her laundry off the line. A white sheet flapped under her outstretched arms. At her feet, a dark-haired little head bobbed above the rim of a basket.

"Tomás." Elizabeth's voice was barely audible.

McQuade lowered her feet to the ground. His throbbing heart found its way into his throat as he watched her take three tentative steps toward her son.

When she saw them, Luisa stepped away from the basket.

"Tomás?" Elizabeth approached slowly and spoke to the child in quiet, melodious Spanish. "Don't be afraid, little one. It's me. It's...it's Mama."

She knelt beside the basket, her white cotton dress billowing around her. Her hands trembled as she reached them, palms up, toward the boy. McQuade shoved his own into the pockets of his jeans, embarrassed even though no one else noticed, that they weren't steady, either. Tomás stood up, holding onto the basket's rim, and looked into his mother's eyes. His own were as big as saucers.

"Do you remember me, Tomás? Will you come to your mama?"

He wrapped a chubby hand around her fingers and searched her hand for some kind of offering. Finding none, he looked into her face again. The rim of the basket failed to support him, and he tottered off balance into his mother's waiting arms.

"Oh, Tomás, I've missed you. I've missed you so much!" The toddler grabbed a handful of his mother's thick hair, and she laughed through joyful tears. "Can you say Mama, little one?"

"Mama?"

"Yes!" She hugged him close and rocked him as she had dreamed of doing for almost a year, while she crooned, "Yes, it's Mama. Yes, yes, yes..."

McQuade watched, sharing her joy, yet distanced from her by it. He'd brought the two of them together, the mother and her son. Elizabeth and Tomás. God, how he wanted to be part of this reunion. It was his reunion, too; he'd made it happen. But he'd lost contact. He stood at the edge of the little yard, saw that Luisa spoke to them, heard their voices, but registered nothing of what was said.

The women would probably find a lot to talk about, he told himself, and he had an appointment with a steak and a bottle of his favorite bourbon. He turned back to the hillside path.

"Sloan!"

Turning again, he squinted into the evening sun.

"Please wait."

"You guys need to get acquainted," he said, somehow managing to speak the words easily. "Take your time. I have to take care of Juanito's account and my stomach. I'll come back for you later if you want."

"We'll take care of them tonight, *señor*," Luisa offered.

Elizabeth took a step toward him, her confusion evident. "Juanito's account is mine to deal with."

"We'll settle up later. Don't worry about it." He nodded at the child in Elizabeth's arms. "Cute kid. He needs looking after. I'll see about a doctor for you. You can plan on an examination before you check out of here, lady."

"Sloan . . ."

"Keep her off that leg," he told Luisa. "I'll check in with you tomorrow, then."

He struck off down the hill, as if steaks really did make appointments and bourbon could really fill the aching hollow in his gut.

* * *

Elizabeth rapped softly on the door to McQuade's room. No answer came. She knew it was early, but she had slipped away before Tomás awoke. She tightened her fist and rapped with more determination.

The suggestion that came from the other side of the door would have been anatomically impossible for her to follow. She was trying to come up with an appropriate reply when the same gruff voice added, "Any comments can be dropped off at the desk."

"I'm afraid I'm speechless, Mr. McQuade."

The next grumble was muffled, and then, "Hold on. Lemme find my pants."

In a moment Elizabeth heard the faucet running. When the door swung open, she could tell that he'd dunked his face in water and hastily combed his hair. "Do you have a watch, lady?"

"No, but I believe it's—"

"Spare me. I've got one. Come on in."

She saw where he'd slept and knew the sheets would still be warm. And she saw, to her relief, that he'd slept alone. His clothes, other than the jeans he wore, were scattered on the floor along with damp towels and several sections of *The Miami Herald*. His pistol lay on the nightstand next to a glass tumbler, which contained the dark remains of a drink.

"Did Felix manage to find you a good steak last night?" she asked.

"Fair."

"And a good bourbon and water?"

"Several."

"Is that why you didn't come back?"

He raked his fingers through his hair and shook his head. "Luisa said they'd look after you, and Tomás was probably confused as it was. He didn't need to deal with another person. He would probably have remembered it was me holding him when he got stuck with a needle."

She smiled. "You'll be surprised. He's not shy. He seems to know me, and he likes Emilio. He won't have any trouble getting used to you—unless, of course, you greet him the way you greeted his mother this morning."

"Yeah, well..." He shrugged. "His mother's got a bad habit of looking me up too early after a rough night."

"Is that so?" She stepped closer to him, then reached up and touched his cheek. "I was beginning to like the beard."

"Yeah?" He smiled, relishing the contact, wanting more. "I thought it looked like hell."

"It was part of the face that chased all my demons away. I owe you such a debt of gratitude, Sloan McQuade." She let her hand slide to his chest, admitting, "Of course, I owe you more than that, on top of what you paid Emilio and Juanito."

He caught her hand in his. She looked up into his eyes and found a curious scowl. "Your debt was canceled when we made love, Elizabeth."

"I don't pay my debts that way." She tried to draw her hand back, but he tightened his grip.

"You know what I mean. I couldn't take money from you now. The advance paid most of the expenses, so let's call it even."

"We aren't even. You did your job. You deserve—"

"I deserve money, right? You needed a little muscle, and I provided that. You didn't always like the looks of it, not when things got muddy and you weren't sure who was wearing the white hat. But I did the job, and I deserve to be paid for it. Is that what you're trying to say?"

"We had an agreement," she reminded him. He was squeezing her hand too hard, but the look in his eyes wasn't threatening. He might have been willing to shoot Juanito, but he wasn't willing to hurt her.

"The terms of the agreement changed somewhere along the way, Elizabeth. Figure it out. We had to bring Tomás home. It wasn't a job anymore. It was the way it had to be."

"Why?"

"Because it was right. Because the kid needed his mother, and because his mother—"

He pierced her with the sharp edge of a glittering scowl, the muscles in his jaw working as he drew a long breath. The look she gave him was as good as an invitation, and he damned himself for wanting one more kiss even as he pulled her into his arms and slanted his mouth across hers. She took his kiss as hungrily as he gave it. He could smell salt air in her hair and a citrusy scent on her skin. Everything about her was clean and fresh, and he wanted the fresh taste of her on his tongue and the feel of her clean hands on his body. He dipped his head to kiss her neck and tangled his fingers in her silken hair.

"Just a simple thank-you, Elizabeth," he whispered into the hollow of her neck. "That's enough."

She flattened her palms against his back and drew herself against him so that he could feel the points of her breasts and the curves of her thighs. "It isn't enough, Sloan. Is it?"

He lifted his head, and she looked up at him, repeating the question almost inaudibly. Without fear, without any reservation, she wanted him. She gave him a look that set his blood on fire.

"God, no," he groaned. "It isn't. Damn you, it isn't."

"Let me give you—"

He lowered her to the bed. There was no time for preliminaries or slow undressing. He pushed her dress aside, and she helped him with his pants. They found each other with trembling hands, touched each other with shuddering need.

"I want—I need to be—"

"Let me love you, Sloan."

"That would be enough," he whispered as he slipped inside her.

"That...oh, yes, that—"

"If you could love me, Elizabeth...oh, honey, if you could love me..."

"I could love no one else," she promised. "Only you."

* * *

Tangled together in sheets and clothing and long black hair, they touched and exchanged soft looks. She wouldn't take the child and leave him now. He wouldn't take the money and run. She touched his lower lip with her middle finger. He smiled and nipped the fleshy pad. It was a time of wonder.

"I want to be touched," she marveled.

"I want to touch you."

"I had forgotten what it was like not to be afraid."

"You know I couldn't hurt you. Not intentionally." He slipped his hand beneath her dress, caressed her belly and cupped her breast. "I want to protect you, Elizabeth. I would do anything to keep you from harm. Go to any lengths."

"But I know you wouldn't have shot an innocent man."

He kissed her hair and said, "No, I wouldn't have," but he knew he was simplifying the matter for her sake. It might be something she would never understand. He'd made a split-second decision to force an issue at the point of a gun. It had been a power play, and he knew she would never sympathize with that. But, unlike the man who'd tormented her, his power was tempered with mercy, with conscience, with the capacity to care. Surely by now she'd learned that much about the man who loved her.

"Where's Tomás?" McQuade asked.

"He was still sleeping when I left. Luisa's probably given him breakfast by now." She snuggled against his shoulder. "I don't want to go back to Miami for a while. I want to stay in this quiet place and get to know my son again." She traced a provocative circle around his flat nipple. "Aren't you due for a vacation, McQuade?"

"I'm due for another advance from you, lady." She raised a questioning eyebrow, and he smiled. "On all that love you promised me. I've got a hell of a lot of it stored up for you."

"Oh, but I'm due for a rest," she teased.

"I haven't forgotten about the doctor, either." He smoothed her hair back and tucked it behind her ear. "And then we're going to collect Tomás from Luisa. You think he'd let me teach him how to swim? Or should I wait a couple of years on that?"

She remembered the dream she'd had of Sloan playing with Tomás on the beach. "I trust your judgment, Sloan." She kissed him and whispered, "I trust you."

Afterword

The islands of De Colores and Arco Iris are lovely figments of the author's imagination. To get to them, one must launch a little boat called *The Silhouette* from the east coast of the Yucatán Peninsula, set a course by the stars and sail straight on till morning.

* * * * *

Look for Kathleen Eagle's first historical romance, PRIVATE TREATY, available in bookstores everywhere this July.

At Dodd Memorial Hospital, Love is the Best Medicine

When temperatures are rising and pulses are racing, Dodd Memorial Hospital is the place to be. Every doctor, nurse and patient is a heart specialist, and their favorite prescription is a little romance. Next month, finish Lucy Hamilton's Dodd Memorial Hospital Trilogy with HEARTBEATS, IM #245.

Nurse Vanessa Rice thought police sergeant Clay Williams was the most annoying man she knew. Then he showed up at Dodd Memorial with a gunshot wound, and the least she could do was be friends with him—if he'd let her. But Clay was interested in something more, and Vanessa didn't want that kind of commitment. She had a career that was important to her, and there was no room in her life for any man. But Clay was determined to show her that they could have a future together—and that there are times when the patient knows best.

ATTRACTIVE, SPACE SAVING BOOK RACK

Display your most prized novels on this handsome and sturdy book rack. The hand-rubbed walnut finish will blend into your library decor with quiet elegance, providing a practical organizer for your favorite hard-or soft-covered books.

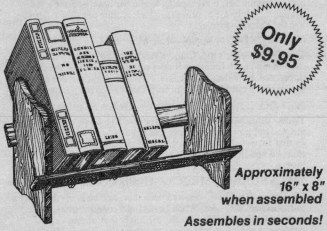

Only $9.95

Approximately 16" x 8" when assembled

Assembles in seconds!

To order, rush your name, address and zip code, along with a check or money order for $10.70* ($9.95 plus 75¢ postage and handling) payable to *Silhouette Books*.

Silhouette Books
Book Rack Offer
901 Fuhrmann Blvd.
P.O. Box 1396
Buffalo, NY 14269-1396

Offer not available in Canada.

*New York and Iowa residents add appropriate sales tax.

BKR-2A

Silhouette Intimate Moments

COMING
NEXT MONTH

#245 HEARTBEATS—Lucy Hamilton

Policeman Clay Williams wanted more than just friendship from Vanessa Rice. But when the drug gang he was after decided to get him by getting her, his campaign to win her heart became a race against time, a battle to prove they had a future together before he lost the chance—forever.

#246 MUSTANG MAN—Lee Magner

To save her father's life, Carolyn Andrews had to find a missing stallion, and only Jonathan Raider could help her. But the search threatened more than their safety. Now that she'd met Jonathan, she knew it would break her heart if they had to say goodbye.

#247 DONOVAN'S PROMISE—Dallas Schulze

Twenty years ago Donovan had promised to take care of Elizabeth forever, but now their marriage was coming to an end. He couldn't let that happen. Somehow he had to prove that his feelings hadn't changed and that the promise he had made once would never be broken.

#248 ANGEL OF MERCY—Heather Graham Pozzessere

DEA agent Brad McKenna had been shot, and he knew that only a miracle could save him. When he regained consciousness, he thought he'd gotten his miracle, for surely that was an angel bending over him. But he soon discovered that Wendy Hawk was a flesh-and-blood woman—and the feelings he had for her were very real.

AVAILABLE THIS MONTH: